The Recruiter

The Recruiter

Alexander Mukte

Three to Five Publishing, LLC

Three to Five Publishing, LLC
2107 N. Decatur Rd., Ste 438
Decatur, GA 30033
www.threetofivepublishing.com

ISBN: 978-1-952030-00-0
ISBN: 978-1-952030-01-7 E-book

For my son. Always remember that you were perfectly designed to be great. Pursue the best version of yourself that you can be, and you will be surrounded by joy, love, and laughter.

Me

Every man must decide whether he will walk in the light of creative altruism or the darkness of destructive selfishness. *This is the judgment.* Life's most persistent and urgent question is, "What are you doing for others?"

Martin Luther King Jr.

Prologue

"Did you think we were going to let you get away with it?" The man's voice was both incredulous and triumphant. The light from the full moon began to fill the room as Ori's eyes adjusted. He inhaled deeply. The man continued as if he was talking to himself, "We knew you were up to something. Did you actually think that you stood a chance?" Ori surveyed the room. He squinted to focus on his surroundings.

"Are you listening to me?" the man continued speaking while Ori remained silent, not acknowledging him. Ori made out three bodies in the room with him: one talking, one holding a flashlight, and a third one close to what looked like the door.

The shack was an old cabin but was well built. No lights were turned on, nor was there a fire burning, so as not to attract any unwanted attention. The natural moonlight was perfect to illuminate most of the space. In the areas where the moonlight did not reach, there was the glow of a bright flashlight. This flashlight was suddenly pointed directly into Ori's eyes.

Chapter 1

Ori didn't get a great night's sleep. He never did when on the verge of closing a new deal or buying a new company. His mind raced through the straights and the curves of why he should or should not go through with the deal. "What am I missing?" he always asked himself. "Do the financials make sense? Are the customers and the market truly there? What about the future potential; where's this industry truly going?" he wondered. "What about the employees? What am I not seeing?" he whispered as he stared at the pages of the *Wall Street Journal*. He scanned through the "What's News" section while his mind continued to work.

It was during moments like these, when Ori could not make up his mind, that his wife would rub his back and say, "Babe, I'm sure you've got a good handle on everything. Trust your gut." Ori often regretted that he let work dictate the course of his marriage, but at the end of the day, the decision was mutual.

He frowned as he thought, *My gut says something isn't right. But Leslie and Roger have always come through for me. Why doubt them now?*

He poured his coffee in his to-go cup and grabbed his green lunchbox off the counter. He was often surprised at how long he kept that lunch box, a free promotional item that his ex-wife gave him several years ago. It wasn't just green; it was a bright, intrusive green. But to Ori, it symbolized something: a simple, humble life in which you appreciated having what you needed and didn't get wrapped up in the distraction of superficial wants. It reminded him to stay grounded and not to take things for granted. He would have been lying if he said it had not also made him think of his wife and the comfortable morning routine they once shared. He smiled wistfully, tossed his lunch bag in the passenger side of his pickup truck, and got on his way.

Ori Clayborn was not the average CEO of a multi-billion-dollar company. He had made it a point to build his business and legacy upon a foundation of doing the right thing and doing right by people. Some teased him for leaving money on the table in negotiations, but in hindsight, his deals had always been hugely successful. Ori's strategy had always been to identify a solution where both parties would win, looking for partners who had the will and desire to be successful together. For him, that made the negotiation process a simple thing. Start with an offer that was beneficial for both parties. After that, it was just discussion, explanation, and going over the fine print. Then they became part of the ecosystem in which they all worked together as one toward sustainable success. As a testament to Ori's success, some had nicknamed him Midas.

The latest deal, however, didn't seem quite right. The Corporate Development Team at Ori's company conducted initial research and identified some operational issues, which could be fixed relatively quickly with the proper systems and employee incentives. The information they were able to gather made the company appear stable. Some of the expenses didn't make sense, but Ori has found that to be typical of family-run companies. In those situations, someone in the family typically used the business as a cash coffer. The company was having some geopolitical challenges in some countries, but nothing that Ori's team hasn't seen before. All in all, pretty typical, so why that nagging feeling?

He hadn't heard anything back from Tony, which struck him as odd. Tony was Ori's preferred information guy and a childhood friend. He kept Tony off the payroll and brought him in as a consultant whenever he felt like he needed either an objective perspective of a situation or if something seemed off and Ori wanted to get to the bottom of it. Ori counted on Tony to explore every angle with the right level of depth and come back with helpful insights delivered in a no-nonsense, direct way. Ori appreciated Tony's directness. Thus, Tony became *the* guy. The only person on Ori's executive team who knew about Tony was Leslie.

Practicing law was in Leslie Ochoa's blood; she came from a long line of attorneys. Her grandparents both provided legal support to the United Farm Workers during the movement in the 1960s, while her parents both worked to rule as unconstitutional Proposition 187, the California initiative that would prevent healthcare to undocumented immigrants. Leslie's family was wary when she decided to work for a corporate law firm. However, with the price tag on Leslie's Harvard Law degree, taking a job in one of the top firms made great financial sense. While there, Leslie climbed the ladder fast, becoming the only female minority partner at the firm. Ori was one of Leslie's earliest clients, and she quickly gained his trust by helping to set up his business while avoiding pitfalls.

The question that kept nagging at Ori about this new lucrative business opportunity was, why him? Why would the owners of this company agree to sell their business to Ori? The founders of the Wesley Corporation started small, with coin laundromats and gas stations in the Midwestern United States. After becoming a hugely successful regional player, they expanded nationally, offering a range of products and services targeted at truckers and travelers, including export and import services.

The Wesley Corporation was an ideal acquisition for Ori for several reasons. First, the laundromat business could be an additional cash cow to fund other research and development initiatives. Second, the export and import infrastructure, although requiring a little work, could help strengthen Ori's global network. *If we can buy the logistical capabilities and not depend on a middleman, this would be great for the company and our customers,* Ori thought to himself.

Lastly, Ori could use the gas station business unit to expand the Project Legacy Initiative, also known as Protect the Legacy Initiative around the office. Ori was especially proud of this initiative which allowed people who were motivated, hardworking, and deserving the opportunity to be their own bosses and gain financial freedom. The initiative used a franchise-type model to help people who qualified to stand up their own business. The options were typically based on opportunities identified by Ori's economic research team to avoid market saturation in any one type of business. Ori's company would provide these entrepreneurs with the business model, training, low-interest financing, and ongoing consulting services to improve the chances of success.

The acquisition of the Wesley Corporation would be a perfect fit and welcome addition to Ori's company. But still, Ori kept wondering, why? Why sell the company to him, or why sell the company at all? The company was founded by the father of Milton and Geoffrey Wesley. After he passed, the brothers continued to build and grow the business as their life's work. Between the two of them, they have three adult children who should be more than capable of continuing to run the business successfully. You'd think that they, too, would want to see their grandfather's business continue to thrive in the family. Numerous companies and private equity firms have tried to purchase them over the years, and the Wesley brothers have always been very clear that their company was not for sale. Ori never even wasted his acquisition team's time in approaching this company, so he found it shocking when Milton Wesley reached out to Roger Garrison, Ori's Chief Financial Officer and Head of Corporate Development, to initiate the meeting.

Ori turned up the radio to stop thinking about work for the remainder of the drive. As he listened to National Public Radio's Morning Edition about the declining death rate and violence in countries that were historically linked to drug trafficking, Ori was reminded how early traffic starts on Atlanta's Ponce de Leon Avenue. When Ori wasn't in a rush, he enjoyed being in the traffic. It allowed him to think about and appreciate the rich history that the city of Atlanta offered.

Parts of the southeastern United States were known for more prevalent racial bigotry. Ori, who had traveled to countless destinations, was no stranger to hearing a derogatory slur or two. He never thought that he would return to the South, let alone call it his home. But the city of Atlanta was something different. Atlanta and its population of half a million people is, in many ways, a beacon of light for diversity and progress. The home of some of the most influential civil rights leaders of both the past and present, Atlanta was one of the few cities where, as a person of color, you had a chance to earn the life you were willing to work for and deserved. As he approached Ponce City Market, he envisioned himself there when it was a Sears, Roebuck & Co. and overlooked the Atlanta Crackers and Black Crackers baseball field, a time well before the Atlanta Braves was even a thought. Ori pondered what those people would have thought if he would have walked up to them and said that in less than one hundred years, your city will be one of the most diverse and visited cities in the country. A melting pot in which people are aware of the history and make conscious efforts to move forward, never forgetting or ignoring the past.

Ori's thoughts shifted as he pulled into the parking lot. He often smirked as he drove by the filled spot labeled "Reserved for Ori Clayborn, CEO." He gave up his parking space to Ms. Hetty, the long-time guard at the front desk. Ori was not into titles and positions, and she was more pleasant if she didn't have to walk far in either cold or hot weather. They worked out an arrangement where she got his parking spot if she and her team allowed him to use the security break room to take a respite whenever needed.

Ori was not like other affluent individuals; he was genuinely self-made. On his mother's side, he descended from slaves, and on his father's side, Ori was a first-generation American. Neither of his parents graduated from college, but both were extremely hard working and very well read. Growing up in that environment taught Ori to be financially conservative because, without a college degree, his parents found it hard to find and keep good-paying jobs. Ori still behaved as if his money could one day stop flowing, even as his success grew.

The funny thing is, no one had caught on yet that *his* car was not parked in that spot. Ms. Hetty's well-cared-for American-made sedan was the type of vehicle that might be expected of a CEO. The vehicle was purchased with the intent of being Ori's company car; he offered it up to Ms. Hetty as part of their deal. Few people knew that their CEO drove a pickup truck with an extended cab. Ori and Ms. Hetty always got a chuckle out of that. Since both were the first in and last out of the office, no one at the company had ever noticed.

As Ori walked toward the elevators, he greeted Ms. Hetty with his usual, "Hi, Ms. Hetty, how's it going today?"

"I can't complain. It's almost Friday, and I'm feeling good. How are you doing today?" She said as she looked up from her computer screen to make eye contact.

"You know, I didn't get much sleep last night, but I can't complain either," he said. "Is it warm in here?" Ori asked, fanning his jacket to catch a cool breeze on his dress shirt.

"Yeah, they are doing something in the vents, so they needed to shut off the air conditioner for a few hours," Ms. Hetty says, leaning into the air flow created by her little portable, oscillating fan.

"Well, stay cool," said Ori, heading for the elevator. "See you later."

Ms. Ross nodded and said, "Alright, you too."

Ori liked Ms. Hetty. She was not college educated, but she was an avid reader. Depending on the time of day, she would be reading something different. Every morning before the crowds started coming in, Ms. Hetty would be reading the national newspaper. Then during her lunch break, she'd be working on the latest weekly edition of the global economic magazine. And at the end of the day, after the office was almost empty, Ms. Hetty would typically be reading a biography of some famous person. When asked why she was always reading, she just answered, "I need to catch up. I learned a while ago that I'm smart. Now I just need to become knowledgeable." Ori couldn't argue with that. Sometimes when he would step away to the security break room, he and Ms. Hetty would start talking, and he was continually surprised by her breadth of interests. Often, Ms. Hetty would enlighten him with insights she'd gained from her reading, keeping Ori on his toes.

Ms. Hetty, now in her sixties, had been happily married for forty years. Her husband and soul mate sadly passed three springs ago. She and her husband had never had kids, and Ori never asked why. What he did know was that they chose to save money so that they could retire early and in style at the age of forty-five and spend the rest of their days traveling. They realized, however, that there might be a lot of downtime between trips. In that downtime, they might drive each other a little crazy, so they decided to find low-pressure work to keep them occupied until the next trip. That is what led Ms. Hetty to find a job at this office building, and she had been working there ever since. Ori considered her a valuable team member whose considerable experience and understanding kept building security running as it should.

Ori settled into his office and spent the next hour or so going through emails and making a list of things on his mind for the day.

"Morning, boss!" Ori looked up to see Leslie in his doorway.

With a smile on his face, Ori replied, "Good morning! How was the show at the Fox last night?"

"The show was great; my date, not so much," Leslie said.

Leslie was a presence that exceeded her actual stature. Her skin was the color of cinnamon, and the freckles on her cheeks gave her heart-shaped face a youthful vibe. She had a broad nose, Cupid's-bow lips, and curly brunette hair that she rarely tried to tame. Her wide-set, mahogany eyes and bright smile made her welcoming and warm when she wasn't on the opposite side of a legal dispute with you.

"I've been reading great reviews," Ori said. "Unfortunate that the guy didn't measure up."

"Well, he didn't make it to the show actually. Halfway through dinner, I discovered that he was uncomfortable being with a woman who's more successful than he is, so I went to the show by myself. I texted Tony to see if he wanted the extra ticket, but he didn't respond."

"Fragile ego, huh? Men," said Ori, shaking his head with a grin. "I fully support your decision. I'm surprised that Tony didn't get back to you. He's always game for a good show," Ori said. "Speaking of Tony, it looks like our Wesley Corporation meeting will be a bit earlier today than expected. They are having breakfast in the corporate dining room. Could you grab Roger for little prep session?"

"Of course," said Leslie as she popped out of the office.

"Thank you!" Ori called after her.

Chapter 2

Leslie always liked meetings in Ori's office. There was so much she wanted to learn about Ori, but she never had the opportunity to talk about anything personal . . . Well, anything personal about Ori. So many times, when they would start a conversation, Leslie had the best intention of extracting some personal information about Ori, but he always gracefully turned the conversation where she would be talking about herself. In fact, she would be divulging some pretty personal information to her boss that she would never have expected. Then, before she knew it, she would be back at her desk realizing that she still did not know one new personal thing about him. Yet, she felt like he was her best friend. So, Leslie made it a point to memorize as much as she could about Ori to share with the employees at his company.

Unlike other executives Leslie knew, Ori did not have university degrees or awards on display. He only had four framed photos. The first was a photo of what looked like a fancy event at the Met or somewhere of equal prestige.

Everyone noticed this photo as it was the first one they passed by when they walked in. The photo was sitting on a beautiful mahogany bookshelf holding a host of books on finance and power, autobiographies of different world leaders, and more. The one book that always stood out to Leslie was Maya Angelou's *I Know Why the Caged Bird Sings*. It happened to be right next to the photo of Ori standing next to a beautiful Oscar-nominated actress that many rumored was his lover. The photo also featured a brilliant-yet-controversial tech billionaire, a well-loved senator from Georgia, the head of the largest bank in the world, and a Saudi royal family member. This image further fueled the rumor that Ori had a vast network, not only consisting of the "Who's Who in Business," but also leading influencers on the global stage.

The next photo hung on a wall behind Ori. It was a black-and-white picture so old that there was a brown tint to it. It appeared to be a young African boy, probably ten or eleven years old, dressed in beads and an elaborate headpiece with a spear and a shield in his hands. Leslie sometimes thought the photo came in the frame. The child looked to be standing at attention but couldn't help smiling as he stood in an exaggerated pose with his shoulders down and back straight. The boy's chin pointed up toward the sky with extreme pride and a grin on his face from ear to ear.

The third sat directly on Ori's desk and only faced him. Leslie caught a glimpse of it once when Roger's assistant accidentally knocked it over when she was bringing something to Ori one day while Leslie was there. Leslie picked it up, but Jordan, Ori's right hand, quickly took the frame from her and placed it back on Ori's desk, positioning it away from his guests. From the few seconds that Leslie saw the photo, it looked like a captured memory of Ori and friends during a hike or camping trip. They were all dressed in outdoor gear and seemed to be wet, which Leslie assumed was from sweating. They all had their arms around each other, and one woman was hanging onto Ori, with her face slightly turned away from the camera. It looked as though she was kissing him on the cheek. Leslie had never seen Ori smile that way.

Few people had ever seen that photo. The main talk was about the picture with the actress, though Leslie found that one more interesting because of Senator Lane Whitman. Although she shouldn't be surprised by Ori's connections, Leslie was impressed that he frequented the same circles of some of the most influential people in the world. Ori was the most approachable boss she'd ever had. She described him to friends and family as the type of person you'd think would run the local hardware store in a Mayberry type of town. There was just a prevailing sense of trust. Most people didn't want to let Ori down. Everyone at the company was pretty stand up too. Ori had a knack for hiring great people. Different personalities and attitudes could clash, but at the end of the day, everyone treated others with respect because they knew that if Ori hired you, then you had kindness in you.

Leslie was skeptical at first, accustomed to quickly discovering the corrupt and crooked side of men, and occasionally of some women. While working as an attorney assigned to some of Ori's business interests, Leslie anticipated the day when she would find out that Ori had some big, dark secret that allowed him to be so successful. "Let's be real," her colleagues used to tell her, "no one starting from his position becomes that wealthy without breaking a few rules." But Leslie trusted Ori. She couldn't explain why, but she just did. He put her at ease, and ever since Leslie started to dedicate more of her time to supporting Ori's business ventures, things in her life just worked out. Leslie's trust in Ori strengthened when he requested that she stop supporting a big case, defending one of the firm's biggest clients, and spend more time starting up one of his nonprofit initiatives. It turned out that case was a career-ender for several of the attorneys. Some people cut corners, people were thrown under the bus, and some of the attorneys on the legal proceeding were disbarred. "It's almost as if Ori knew how that case would end and looked out for me," Leslie recalls, as she told one of her colleagues the details of the corrupt activities.

The fact that Ori rubbed elbows with billionaires and world leaders caught most people off guard; he didn't seem like that type of person. After Leslie worked at the company for a bit, she noticed that some of those people would come through the office for a visit, notably the senator. She assumed he was always around to get a sneak peek of the latest technology or to talk about campaign donations. The two went out to lunch occasionally, and Leslie heard frequent references to Senator Whitman hosting Ori for dinner. Ori seemed apolitical, so it was a surprise that he was such good friends with this senator. It was probably a good thing since everyone thought that this senator would be the next president of the United States.

Leslie could not say anything negative about the senator; the few interactions she had with him were positive. However, she always questioned his background, or rather his family's background. His family became wealthy from predatory lending and aggressive real estate tactics that tended to negatively impact people of lower socioeconomic status. Senator Lane Whitman, by all accounts, was a breath of fresh air for that family and their legacy, though Leslie wasn't quite sure how to feel about the positive light the senator always tried to shine on his family legacy. It's hard to distance oneself from that kind of reputation, especially when you're in the public eye. She wouldn't expect him to condemn the business of his father and grandfather, but still. Aside from that, Lane's brother ran the family business, and Ori's company competed with them in some markets. That's why Leslie found the relationship between Senator Whitman and Ori particularly peculiar.

Leslie grabbed Roger, and they returned to Ori's office together.

In the office, Roger was eager to talk. A very mild-mannered man, Roger was brimming with enthusiasm. "Ori, I had breakfast with the Wesley brothers this morning, and they are good guys. They are excited to sell the business to us; they think that we are the right people to take their business to the next level."

A slim man, Roger had a small belly that he tried his best to hide. His full beard was always impeccably maintained, and he had carefully styled hair. Even though there was a loose dress code in the office, Roger always wore a stylish, yet conservative, suit and tie. He looked the part of someone born to wealth, but his parents were both public school educators. He always said they taught him how to be excellent at managing his money. He attended top tier colleges for both his undergraduate degree as well as his MBA. His measured manners, prominent brow bridge, and steely blue eyes gave some the false impression that he was unapproachable.

Ori leaned forward with a smile. "That's great to hear. Have you been able to gauge why it is that they are willing to sell?"

Roger responded, "They haven't said outright, but I get the feeling that they are just ready to cash it in. They've done well from this company and feel like they can maximize the sale price now while they are ahead. Also, after spending some time with their kids last month, I would not have much confidence in their ability to take the company forward." The smile slowly leaves Roger's face. "Why do you ask?"

"Something just doesn't seem right to me," Ori said, looking out his office window.

"What's concerning you?" asked Roger.

"It seems all too easy. These guys are smart businessmen with the means to keep growing the company. Selling a lucrative family company with this much potential doesn't seem like a move these guys would make. Maybe their children aren't prepared or able to take over the business from them now, but who's to say that won't change? Or, they could hire someone external to run the business and still maintain ownership," Ori said. "There are other options."

"Well," Roger broke the silence, "You are right. They've done some incredibly brilliant things to grow their business. The Wesley brothers were pioneers, in a sense. Maybe there's a strategic play somewhere. Maybe they want the cash to go after the next big idea. Or maybe they'll surprise me and back out. It's not uncommon that owners of good family-run companies change their minds during the final negotiations. But what they keep saying is that you, Ori, are the man they think will do great things with what their family has built."

"Maybe," Ori said, still looking out of the window. "Maybe they will still agree to sell their company to us under our terms. How much time do we have before our meeting?"

"About an hour," replied Roger.

"All right, you better get back with them," Ori said.

As Roger and Leslie got up to leave, Ori shifted his gaze from the window to Leslie. "Do you have another second, Leslie?"

Leslie turned. "Sure, what's up?"

"No new information on them from Tony?"

"I haven't heard anything back yet," Leslie said.

"That's so odd. Tony always delivers." Ori paused. "And he's never late."

The room was quiet for a few seconds, both thinking about the perplexity of the situation.

"I've learned to question things that come so easily in this world." Ori said as he looked back out of the window, "It's just odd that the deal of a lifetime happens to fall into our laps. I can't help but wonder what invisible strings are attached."

Leslie considered this and responded, "You're always reminding me to trust my gut. Let's hear them out. If you don't like what they are saying, then we walk away."

Jordan, Ori's executive assistant, entered the office to run through the daily and weekly schedule. She reminded him that the meeting to review the deal with the Wesley Corporation was moved up to the morning, citing that Milton and Geoffrey have personal conflicts and need to return home earlier than planned.

Jordan was always an enigma to Leslie, as well as to most employees at the company. She was only around when Ori was present. And she would only take instructions or polite requests from Ori.

Jordan's athletic build and radiant, bronze skin were the envy of many. Her short, black hair and androgynous look topped off her appealing features. Jordan was stoic and made a point to say as few words as possible. Her physical features often led people to mistake her for a young college intern. However, upon peering into her pale green eyes, you got an overpowering sense that she knew things that you couldn't even begin to comprehend.

Leslie commented, "I wish we could have kept the original time; maybe that would have given Tony enough time to get back to us with something."

"Yeah, but he doesn't typically cut it down to the wire like this," Ori said.

"Do you think we need to worry?" Leslie asked, visibly concerned.

Ori smiled, an attempt to ease Leslie's worries. "If Tony were in any trouble, he knows how to handle himself. I'm sure there's nothing serious, and there's probably some funny story behind all of this."

"Do you need anything for this meeting?" Jordan asked.

"Can you make sure that we are in the smaller conference room?" Ori asked.

"Of course. I'll get it prepared and let Roger know," Jordan said, and she walked out of the office.

"Why change to the smaller conference room?" Leslie asked.

"It has more windows and nice views. I tend to have better conversations in there," Ori said.

Leslie loved to watch Ori work. One of Leslie's courses in her Executive MBA program was all about emotional intelligence. As an attorney, she never thought that much about it. She even laughed at the course after reading the syllabus, thinking it would be a fluffy class. Leslie cared a great deal for her work and her clients when she was an attorney. She focused on the outcomes for her clients and underestimated the power of being emotionally intelligent. But she had really come to value it. Ori understood people. He made it a habit to learn how they worked and what motivated them. That's one of the things that made Ori effective.

Once she started attending the classes, she understood what Ori was doing and why it was successful. He not only had the business and strategic intellect, but he was extraordinary on an interpersonal level with all different types of people. He understood how people worked and what they needed. It was a gift. After being around people for a few minutes, Ori could make them feel like he had known them for their entire lives. Then, when the time was right, he would ask his questions. Soft skills are what they call them, and Ori mastered them. Ori had a way of making everyone feel important, even sometimes more important than he was. On top of that, Ori had vision and integrity. He was a rarity when most leaders were followers of others, yet he was known to stay true to his moral compass, unapologetically. Leslie hadn't found a company that was on the same ethical page as her, not until Ori's company.

As Ori walked Leslie out of his office, they stopped in the doorway to allow the Wesley Corporation representatives to pass, with Roger leading the way, speaking with Milton Wesley.

The two Wesley brothers were barrel-chested men, about average height in their mid-to-late fifties or early sixties. They both had white, nicely combed hair with facial features so similar that they could have been mistaken for twins. However, there were a couple of clues that could be used to tell the brothers apart. Geoffrey was a few inches taller than Milton, and while they lived in the same city and had the same profession, they looked as if they came from different worlds. Geoffrey dressed conservatively for meetings, typically in a charcoal or navy blue suit, always with a tie. Milton, on the other hand, was more the flashy type. He sported a tan and often donned a nice pair of jeans and a sports coat.

The group stopped briefly for Geoffrey and Milton Wesley to greet Ori and Leslie. They all quickly exchanged pleasantries and comments on the promise of the upcoming discussion.

"That's a bigger group than I would have imagined," Leslie said as they watched the last of the entourage vanish around the corner toward the small conference room.

"Yes," Ori said, clearly in thought. "I recognized some of them, but there was a new face or two in the group."

"Do you think they brought in consultants?" Leslie added.

"Maybe," Ori said. "I guess it's almost time to find out. Let's not keep them waiting. I'll just grab my jacket."

Ori put on his jacket, then he took two cell phones from the desk, one a new model and the other an older flip phone, and put one in each inside jacket pocket.

"Can I ask you something?" Leslie said.

"Sure," Ori said.

"Of all this time we've worked together . . ." Leslie paused. "I've never seen you on that second phone. Never a text message or a call. Why do you have it?"

Ori smiled with a hint of nostalgia in his eye. "I've had this number for a very long time. The people who have this number are those that I want to ensure can reach me directly if they need me."

Chapter 3

In the meeting room, Leslie was surprised by the different faces in attendance. The Wesley brothers brought some people that she had expected to come: both Milton and Geoffrey were there, the corporate attorneys, their CFO, and the head of the board of directors. None of the Wesley children were in attendance. There were, however, two new faces on the deal team who were sitting in chairs along the wall. Leslie knew everyone who signed the nondisclosure agreements, and these two gentlemen were new faces.

One of the men's attire was a little too flashy for a consultant; Leslie recognized the five-thousand-dollar Tom Ford suit. Plus, Geoffrey was notorious for a maniacal focus on spending wisely. If these were consultants, Geoffrey would not approve.

She heard Ori's voice cut through her mental assessment of the man's outfit. "Have we met before?" Ori asked.

"I'm afraid not. I'm Nicolas Villalobos," the man said, with a thick Latino accent, extending his hand to shake Ori's.

This man's presence gave Leslie pause. She would have remembered someone with this name on the list submitted to receive and sign a nondisclosure agreement. Leslie liked to take note of diversity among senior executives at large companies.

Nicolas stood around five feet, nine inches tall, and despite being sharply dressed, Leslie could tell he had a very thin frame. Leslie knew the look of someone skilled at hiding his addiction from people not really trying to find it. And then there were his red-rimmed eyes. In most circumstances, Leslie would default to an assumption that this was an ambitious employee surviving off the minimum required hours of sleep—the look that's traditionally associated with investment bankers and management consultants. Something told her that was not the case here, although he did look like he could have come out of an investment bank. She tried to tuck her initial assessment away and told herself maybe he was part of the investment team.

The other man, with short, dirty-blonde hair, simply responded, "It's a pleasure to meet you. Thank you for having us down."

Leslie prided herself on reading people and situations, and this was one reason she was so successful at her previous law firm. She often thought back to what Ori told her when he offered Leslie the job, "You see through things. You see past what people want to show you. That makes you good. Keep that up, develop that skill, and you'll get better. But . . . once you can see past yourself, see beyond what you are allowing to show yourself, then you will progress on your journey to greatness."

Ori finished shaking everyone's hands and made his way to the empty seat between Jordan and Leslie. To kick the meeting off, Ori welcomed both the brothers and introduced his team, allowing each person to say a word about himself. Then the Wesley brothers followed suit, as did their attorneys, CFO, and the board members.

Ori looked at the individuals behind the Wesley brothers and their team. "And you, gentlemen? Please pull up a chair and introduce yourselves." Nicolas Villalobos shifted in his chair uneasily, and looked at his colleague for a reaction.

"I never caught your name," Ori said to the second gentleman.

"I'm Silas. I'm in charge of government affairs and public relations," Silas said as he pulled his chair up to the table. Nicolas followed him.

Silas stuck out from the rest of the group. Standing well over six feet tall, he had a durable build, but not one you would get from squatting and bench pressing in front of a mirror at the gym. He had more of a rugged, athletic look.

His shoes and suit were appropriate, yet not too flashy. His watch confirmed Leslie's suspicion of an active outdoor lifestyle. It was a Citizen's watch, with a black face and a band made of titanium. It was not the type of watch Leslie was used to seeing on people in government affairs roles, with the trend toward smart technology. Leslie, still hesitant about the idea of having a piece of technology track every step she took, appreciated when someone was wearing a traditional watch.

"Now that we are all acquainted . . .," Roger said, as he transitioned to the true content of the meeting. He opened by reiterating the exciting potential of becoming one company. He gave a nod to some of the successes and strengths of the Wesley Corporation. As Roger concluded his opening remarks, he turned to Ori to share a few words. Leslie had seen Ori do this sort of setup a hundred times. He generally had a few solid talking points written down and planned, but he seemed to hesitate.

Ori set the talking points to the side, looked back and forth between Milton and Geoffrey, and asked, "Why now, and why us? I don't mean to offend you, but I'm having trouble understanding why. Why sell such a great company, and why trust us so explicitly with it?" Some people in the room squirmed, and the brothers looked both at each other and Roger with what looked like surprise and confusion.

"Leslie and her team," Ori said gesturing to Leslie, "have done a significant amount of research. We know how family-oriented you all are."

Leslie averted her eyes from Milton as she recalled the extramarital exploits in his background check.

Ori continued, "You have adult children who could keep the business in your family for future generations. Why would you just let it go?"

As Ori finished this question, Roger jumped in, "I mean, don't get us wrong. We would love to buy your company. You are smart men, so we know you are fully aware of what you are giving up. But we would like to understand why."

Ori added, "Everything I do and everything I build is meant to be left for future generations." Ori shifted his gaze between the Wesley brothers. "If I had what you have, I wouldn't give it away."

After looking at his brother for a few seconds, Geoffrey, the pensive and methodical man that he is, began, "As you've combed through the financials, I'm sure you have come to understand that we may have spoiled our kids. They've grown up thinking that they don't have to work and can get everything they want with ease. I don't trust that they will do the right thing with what we leave them. Additionally, they've made some questionable business decisions that have made us conclude that our company and our legacy would be better off run as a part of your company. We know your track record; we know how fair your deals are and how well you take care of the employees in the companies you acquire." His eyes started to get a little misty. "Our family and this company have provided generations of families with great jobs, money to buy homes, put their kids through college, and retire happily. Selling to you won't change that, and it will provide opportunity for the next generations of our family to get back on the right path."

"The right path." A curious phrase to use, Leslie thought. Everyone is a work in progress, and new leaders commonly happen down the wrong path, but it's usually not something they can't come back from. It saddened her that a man like Geoffrey felt that his own kids were a lost cause.

"I'm truly sorry to hear that, but your message is understood. We think that there's a lot of good we can do with the great business that you built," Ori replied.

"So, what's next? How do we move forward?" Milton said excitedly.

Roger started, "You've had a chance to learn about our company and our culture, but do you have any outstanding questions for us?"

Both Geoffrey and Milton shake their heads.

"Well," Leslie said, "now the fun begins. We will create an initial draft of the contract. Typically, the contract negotiations will last several weeks to several months, depending on how complex the deal is. We'll start working on this paperwork and get it to your legal team in the next few weeks."

Chapter 4

As Ori, Leslie, and team escorted the Wesley Corporation representatives out of the conference room, Geoffrey made a comment to Ori, "I must say that I am very impressed by your approach to business. It's unconventional in today's environment, but it seems to be successful."

"Did Roger give you a tour and explain more about how we operate?" Ori asked.

"He did, but I'd still like to know more of the full picture. You acquire different companies in a wide range of industries, like a conglomerate, but I don't understand how you gain any efficiency in scale or operations." Geoffrey paused, realizing how his words may have sounded. "I don't mean to cause you any offense, and again from the looks of things," Geoffrey motions his hands around the floor to the beautiful building and all of the employees, "your model seems to be working very well for you. I'm curious to better understand how."

"I understand from the outside looking in all of the acquisitions we make seem to be random, but if you take a few steps back to understand the full picture, I assure you that they all make sense with what we are trying to accomplish," Ori said.

"Roger may have explained this already, so forgive me for repeating anything that you may have heard, but one of my early creations was a crowdsourcing type of software for small businesses. This system allows every small business using the software to be viewed as one large retailer when it comes to ordering products to sell to their customers or for ordering raw materials to create their products."

"Your software is a procurement tool that allows small businesses to order goods. That's not really a novelty," Milton said.

Ori smiled. "Yes, allowing small businesses to quickly assess what supplies are running low and to quickly reorder them by a click of a button is not new at all. You are correct. The key is that our algorithms pool all of that data together quickly so that when the business owner needs to order more supplies, her order is combined with the orders of millions of other small business owners."

"Think of it as a type of co-op model," Leslie interjects.

"That's right," Ori said excitedly. "Members sign up to use our software and combine their orders with the other members' orders."

"I see," Geoffrey said. "As you get more members in your co-op combining their orders, then you have enough volume to get discounted prices from manufacturers."

"Exactly," Ori said. "That's how we started, with a mission of giving the small business owner a fighting chance against the giant retailers. Most consumers in our country make their purchases based on price and convenience, even if it is at their own detriment. I had a vision that if we could figure out a way for Ms. Ella's corner store to have the same products at the same prices as the big-box stores, then her community would continue to support her business. Then that money stays in her community."

"But why take on so much risk? You own fast-food chains and . . ."

Ori interjects, "Healthy fast-food chains."

"Yes, healthy fast-food chains," Geoffrey corrects himself. "Pharmacy chains, grocery stores. I even read somewhere that you are exploring buying an apparel company."

"What we own here at corporate is the manufacturing arm of the different industries you've mentioned. Going back to the retail store example, we noticed that we could get better margins for our members if we owned some of the manufacturing of more popular items. It's like any business model. We began to branch out of the retail store space when we realized other areas where money was leaving the community. That's why it made sense for us to stand up similar models in the pharmacy, grocery store, and restaurant spaces, and so on. We do not have any intention to purchase an already established apparel company. We have plenty of members who design and create their own very stylish clothing, shoes, and accessories. We've recently created some joint ventures with apparel manufacturers who can mass-produce our members' items, and they will be marketed and sold in our member stores."

"How do you make money? It seems like you are taking on a lot of unnecessary risks," Milton said.

"All of our members pay a fee for being a part of the system," Roger said. "Also, we provide very low-interest financing to people who want to stand up their own business as well."

"The more members and different businesses you have, the more your revenue?" Geoffrey asked.

"That is correct," Roger said.

Ori added, "Really, our success is an indicator of our members' success. My vision for this entire enterprise was to stand up a business model where everyone could be successful. I will admit that it will be challenging for any of our members to become billionaires, but if my theory holds true, then they all have a shot at being financially independent. We do have requirements of all our members as well."

"What kind of requirements?" Silas asked, speaking up for the first time since the meeting.

Leslie said, "We require that our members, for example, pay their employees a wage that we find fair, that they use one of our pre-approved service providers, that they offer training and development to their employees and offer performance-based bonuses."

"We also request that all of our members have a family-first focus when it comes to work and life," Ori said. "Our members need to make sure that they are living healthy lives and that their families are living healthy lives too."

"This sounds nice, but why would you or anyone do this?" Silas asked.

"Because I can," Ori said sharply. After a brief, uncomfortable pause, Ori softened his tone. "And because someone should. Don't get confused, gentlemen; I'm not solely doing this out of the kindness of my heart. I'm doing this to prevent a problem that will impact all of us if it's not taken care of."

"What problem is that?" Silas asked.

"Indentured servitude," Ori said, pausing slightly before continuing. "Or something of the sort. Did you know that the student debt in our country is around one-point-four trillion dollars? Don't get me wrong, I believe that a good education is essential. However, I don't think that it makes sense for it to cost a hundred thousand dollars for a degree, especially when in many cases, the salary coming out might be less than half that. But here's what I'm really worried about. The United States of America has always been the land of opportunity. It's the only place that I know of where the kid of an immigrant can one day become the president. The US is a beacon of hope and possibility. If that light fades, then I fear the world will become a dark place."

"Our business model is set up to allow people to own something. A lot of people have been led to believe that the way they make it is to work hard for someone else. We want to give them the opportunity to work hard for themselves." Ori paused for a minute, then continued. "I understand how some people don't see this as their problem. If you've been fortunate enough to be able to save money for your kids, then you don't think you have anything to worry about. But let me put it to you this way: if eighty percent of the nation is broke, desperate, and hopeless, how long do you think it will be before they get fed up and take aim at the twenty percent who have everything? It may not be during our generation, or even during our children's generation, but that poverty gap is only widening, and it's just a matter of time—a matter of time before our society is torn apart and the nation that we know and love is destroyed. So, Silas, I hope I did a sufficient job of answering your question as to why I chose to do what I'm doing."

"You're an idealist."

"Why, Silas, you make it sound like it's a bad thing," Ori said with a smile.

Silas looked pensive and fell back to trail them.

Ori and Geoffrey then engaged in small talk about their weekend plans. Geoffrey glanced back at Milton and Roger, who were in an animated conversation. Geoffrey looked back at Ori and said, "I'm sure that you can imagine that I'm a very well-connected man, and I've looked into you. I've never heard a bad word about you. Everyone I've spoken with has said that you are a good man and an honest man who keeps his word."

Geoffrey reached out to shake Ori's hand. "If that's true," he said as he glanced over to Nicolas and Silas who were staring at him, "I wish you good luck with the due diligence." After shaking Ori's hand firmly, both men gave each other a nod.

Almost immediately, Geoffrey turned to his brother and Roger. "Alright guys, I am still feeling the drinks from last night, so let's get to the airport and get me home." Geoffrey turned to Leslie. "Thank you for your work with our legal team to get all of this paperwork together. I'm looking forward to working with you."

After everyone had a final handshake and said their goodbyes, the two brothers and their entourage walked down the hall and disappeared behind the elevator doors.

As Ori, Leslie, and Roger walked back toward their offices, Ori said, "Anybody feel like a walk through research and development? There's something new I want to show you."

"I'm in!" Leslie said. She loved getting to go behind the glass, which is not an everyday thing for her in Legal.

Roger lifted his eyebrows in intrigue and said, "Sure thing."

The trio made their way to the frosted double glass doors. They could vaguely see figures moving around on the other side.

Ori placed one finger on the glass door. As soon as his skin touched the glass, Leslie heard the latch unhinging. She didn't know the details of each of the emerging projects, but she did know that this entire floor specialized in developing products that connect technology with physical and metaphysical human characteristics. The group walked through the door, and Ori looked at one of the lab technicians. "Are we able to use the prototype conference room?"

"Of course," the technician replied.

"Great, thank you," Ori responded. The group walked into a large conference room that looked almost exactly like the room they were in earlier with the Wesley Corporation. The walls were made of transparent glass, and the room contained a large wooden table with eight chairs surrounding it. "Privacy please," Ori said, seemingly talking to the room. As soon as he said it, the transparent glass converted to the opaque frost like that of the entrance to the lab.

Ori started, "This is something I'm really excited about. It's still a long way from entering the market, but this is what the team is calling an energy room."

The lights in the room started to slowly dim until the room was entirely black. "This room is configured to my personal settings right now, but it could be synced with anyone."

"Leslie," Ori said, "why don't you touch the glass and think about what you want the room setting to be?"

She does as asked, and without ever saying a word, the lights slowly turn back on so that the room has a low dim setting. Leslie audibly gasped.

"Thank you, Leslie. Now will you please think of something else?" Ori said.

"Sure," Leslie responded with wonder.

"Wait," Roger said. "How do you change who has control?"

"For anyone who hasn't used the room or system before, he or she would just need to touch the glass as Leslie did. Why don't you try and think of one thing that you want to project on the screen?"

An image started to appear on the glass wall as if someone had turned on a projector. It's a video of a young man, in his mid-twenties, wearing a rock and roll t-shirt. He's jamming, singing at the top of his lungs.

"Whoa! This is incredible," Roger said.

"Was that you?" asked Leslie.

"That was my brother. Wild, I know, right? He and I were just reminiscing about the concerts we used to go to together. Been a long time," Roger said.

As soon as he removed his finger, the video went away, and the lights in the room came on.

"We've figured out a way to interact directly with dark energy and dark matter," Ori explained.

"I'm going to need more explanation than that." Leslie laughed.

"Fair enough," Ori said as the room turned completely dark. A small, circular yellow light appeared on the black glass, and it quickly grew. It was an image of the sun as well as the planets rotating around it. The image zooms in on planet Earth. "All the matter that we know of makes up less than five percent of the universe. This includes our planet, our solar system." As Ori said this, the image of Earth on the glass wall shrank as the glass wall became a giant image of the Milky Way. "This also includes our galaxy, as well as every other galaxy in existence."

"Umm, what?" Roger said, trying to comprehend.

"Yes, that's right," Ori said while the glass walls turned pitch black. "There are still a lot of unknowns about dark energy and dark matter, but we do know that they make up roughly ninety-five percent of the universe. We also know that the vast blackness that brilliant minds thought was nothing but just space is actually something intricate that ties us all together." Just as Ori said this, the black area surrounding the galaxies turned into one massive neon-colored web-like structure, seamlessly connecting every galaxy and blank space on the screen. "We may not be able to see it, but something is definitely out there, holding all of this together. This technology works to capture and harness this energy."

The lights in the room turned back on as Ori continued. "We are still exploring all of the possibilities of channeling this energy, but so far, we have discovered a viable conductor. Several of our patents are actually for technology that allows us to develop, store, and distribute dark energy." Ori looked around at the screen. "But this is actually showing potential to leverage dark energy to bring unconscious thoughts and ideas to life."

"How long until this technology will be ready for the market?" Roger asked.

"It could be years, or it could never be," Ori said, making eye contact with Leslie. "Not every innovation is meant to be put in the hands of man."

Chapter 5

Ori had a weekly briefing meeting with his leadership team. After they wrapped up, he and Roger walked out at the same time. Ori turned to Roger. "What are you doing for lunch today?"

"No plans," Roger said as they turned and walked toward their offices.

"Let's go grab some Korean tacos," Ori said.

"Sounds good," Roger replied.

"Leslie," Ori called over his shoulder, before turning to look at her, "are you down for some Korean tacos too?"

"I'm always game," Leslie said. "I just need to send one more e-mail, and then I'll meet you downstairs."

While downstairs, Roger and Ori waited at Ms. Hetty's station for Leslie. "Ms. Hetty, we're going to get some Korean tacos. Do you want me to pick up some for you too?" Ori asked.

"From which spot, the place down the street or the one across town?" Ms. Hetty asked with a suspicious look.

"The place across town, of course," Ori said.

"Well, Mr. Roger likes to go to the other place sometimes," Ms. Hetty replied.

"Ha, well not on my watch," Ori said as he smirked. "So, should I get your usual?"

"Yes, please," Ms. Hetty said as she started pulling money out of her purse.

Ori looked at Ms. Hetty. "You'll need to let me pay one of these days."

"Baby, I don't want to owe anyone anything," Ms. Hetty said with feeling. "Making debt a habit is how they get you."

"Who is 'they'?" Roger asked.

Ori and Ms. Hetty smiled and just shook their heads. Roger shrugged and decided to let it go. The elevator dinged, and Leslie walked out to join them.

They turned to walk out of the building with Ori leading the way. Roger asked, "Ori, are you actually going to drive us today?"

Ori said with a laugh in his voice, "Of course not. I just know you're parked in the same spot as always." They then heard Ms. Hetty call after them. "Ori! Someone is on the phone for you. They say it's urgent."

"It can't be that urgent if they didn't call your cell, right?" Roger said.

"They're saying it can't wait," Ms. Hetty said.

"Everything is always urgent," Ori said, "but it's never the end of the world. Please get their number and tell them I'll call them back. I need to eat."

As the group turned to continue walking to the parking lot, they felt a rough vibration, milliseconds before they heard a loud and profound boom. The windows on the ground floor of the building shattered, and the fire alarm started blaring.

Chapter 6

Leslie's ears were ringing as she began to regain her senses. She saw Ori kneeling over her. His lips were moving, but she was having trouble making out his words. Slowly she realized he was asking, "Are you ok?" She nodded feebly, and he extended his hand to pull her up to sitting.

Panic rose in her chest. She must have blacked out. She started looking around, trying to piece together what happened and if everyone was ok. Past Ori she saw fire and smoke coming from a car. And a few feet away from him, she saw Roger sitting and holding his head. She realized there was a pounding in her own head as well.

Ori touched her shoulder, and she realized he was saying something else to her. She tried to focus. "We've got to get you and Roger inside where it's safe," Ori was saying.

"Isn't that your car?" Leslie asked.

"Don't worry about it; everything is ok. We need to get inside where it's safe," Ori said.

"What about Ms. Hetty?" Leslie asked.

"She's okay; she was inside the building," Ori said. "Are you ok to stand up?"

Leslie noticed that Roger made his way over to her and extended his hand to help her up.

Leslie took both of their hands, and the two men helped her to her feet.

Jordan appeared as well as a flood of other employees. Ori yelled, "Everyone, stay in the building, away from the windows. Jordan, call the police."

Chapter 7

Special Agent Mikiko Shikibu opened Special Agent Evelyn Blackwood's door abruptly. "Hey, Evelyn, you're needed in the large conference room immediately."

Evelyn looked at her computer. "I don't see anything on my calendar."

"This just came up," Mikiko said, seeming a little out of breath. "Deputy Director Chisholm and Section Chief Appleton are waiting."

"Do you know what this is about?" Evelyn asked. The last time Deputy Director Chisholm was in a briefing was when there was the suspicion that rogue Russian agents had influenced several election results. "She doesn't typically get involved in briefs unless there's a pretty serious situation."

Mikiko just shook her head and led the way.

As Evelyn walked into the briefing room, three well-known faces appear on a large screen covering the wall.

"Thank you for joining us, ladies," Section Chief Appleton said with an annoyed tone.

Section Chief Appleton was notorious throughout the organization for being a prick. He had burned every bridge imaginable but somehow found a way to continually advance. The only thing he had going for him was that he looked the part of an FBI agent. Appleton was tall, his dirty-blonde hair always neatly combed, and his skin freshly shaved. You would never see the section chief without a suit and tie. Other agents joked that if he went to the gym, he'd probably wear a tie there too.

Evelyn did not acknowledge the section chief's comment as she surveyed the room to see who all was in attendance. In addition to Section Chief Appleton and Deputy Director Chisholm, Evelyn noticed a few analysts that she had worked with on different joint task force initiatives. She also recognized Special Agent Richard Cramer, one of the section chief's lackeys.

Agent Cramer came from a long line of West Point graduates and had relatives who had fought in every single American and British war. If his fiery red hair and fair skin didn't give away his Irish ancestry, then the forearm tattoos of the American and Irish flags peeking out of rolled-up shirt sleeves certainly did.

The final attendee in the room was Special Agent Jake Chivington. Evelyn had heard of him but had never worked on a case with him. He was known as one with high potential in the agency, someone being groomed by Deputy Director Chisholm. Seeing him in the room gave

Evelyn a familiar knot in her stomach that she could never ignore, a feeling that always meant she needed to be alert.

Agent Chivington had short, dark brown hair that was always unkempt and sunken eyes that Evelyn thought made him look like he was tired. Mikiko, as well as every other person who preferred the company of men, described Chivington as the sexiest agent in the Bureau. But his track record was questionable. She could never understand why most of the cases he worked on ended up going south. The Deputy Director must have always assigned him the toughest cases to work, the no-win situations. Evelyn had always been impressed by Chisholm's intellect, and Evelyn is not easily impressed. If the Deputy Director saw something in Chivington, working this case together would be a good way to learn what that something was.

"God, he gets on my nerves," Mikiko whispered, referring to Section Chief Appleton.

Mikiko was one of those bridges that Appleton had burned. Mikiko and then Agent Appleton were working on an assignment that led them to Central America. Mikiko specialized as an economist and data scientist. Her skills were necessary for that mission, but something went wrong. According to Mikiko, Appleton betrayed her. Mikiko was removed from the assignment. There were rumors that part of the mission required the two to go deep undercover as a couple. Mikiko never gave Evelyn any details, and out of respect for her friend's wishes, Evelyn had never pressed it further.

Mikiko was petite and spunky. Evelyn often joked that Mikiko had the metabolism of an adolescent since she could eat anything and everything in sight without ever gaining a single pound. Mikiko had shoulder-length, glossy black hair which she often wore in a tight bun. The male agents would have a few drinks and drool over her. Evelyn lost count of the number of times someone asked her to set him up with Mikiko on a date. Evelyn marveled at how most of the compliments Mikiko received were tied to her appearance. The first reason was that she didn't flaunt it. The second was how brilliant Mikiko was. When they were roommates in the academy, they often talked about how the two of them would run the Bureau one day, and Evelyn felt like they had the abilities to do just that.

"Agent Shikibu," Appleton said, "am I interrupting something?"

Mikiko did not respond; she looked at Appleton with her head tilted high and gestured back at the screen as a signal for him to continue.

"As I was saying, who can tell me who these three individuals are?" Appleton asked, not breaking his stare at Mikiko.

"Jason Jimenez out of New York, Mike aka 'Mikey' Romano out of Chicago, and the notorious Victor aka 'Big Vick' Ward out of Los Angeles. They are suspected to be the heads of the largest crime syndicates in the US," said an eager analyst from the other side of the briefing room.

"Do any of you know what these three have in common?" Appleton asked.

The room was quiet. The analysts looked around to see who would come up with the right answer or who would have the nerve even to speak up. They all knew of the section chief as a hard-ass who thinks that he is the smartest person in the room and who will brutally embarrass anyone who is incorrect. He loved to test people's knowledge, asking challenging questions to which he already knew the answers.

"You," Appleton called out an analyst, "What do you think these three have in common?" Appleton enjoyed putting people on the spot.

"Uh, uh," the analyst stammered.

"Uh, uh, uh," Appleton said in a mocking tone. "Why are you even in here? Go grab me some coffee!" he barked.

He turned back to Mikiko. "Agent Shikibu, you had a lot to say earlier. What do you have to say now?"

Evelyn hated bullies, and she especially hated it when bullies were picking on her friends. She noticed Mikiko turning red from frustration, and Evelyn decided to interrupt.

"Let me have a crack at it," Evelyn said. "There are a few things that these three men have in common." Evelyn tilted her head to stare directly at Appleton. "Let's see what answer would appease you. We have already established that they are all alleged drug kingpins. Next up, they all have similar money laundering and distribution networks in addition to overlapping financial connections. But that's well known, at least in our circles. The type and quality of drugs that they put on the street are similar, so there's the potential that they all use the same supplier. They all brutally dominate and run their territories, so that might also suggest they have protection."

"Is that all?" Appleton tried to interrupt, but the deputy director put up her hand to stop him.

Something started clicking in Evelyn's brain. She narrowed her eyes, stood up and walked closer to the screen. She began talking out her train of thought, mostly for herself, but bringing the room along.

"There was a brief spike in gang-related chatter and violence not too long ago. It all stopped abruptly after a few ruthless killings of some pretty high-level soldiers in these three syndicates. There has not been any chatter around these three for . . ." Evelyn paused as she sorted through her realization.

Evelyn turned and said confidently, "They are all missing."

"That's exactly right, Agent Blackwood," Deputy Director Chisholm said with a smile.

Appleton continued, clearly frustrated that his fun had been ruined, "The fact that these three thugs are missing isn't necessarily something to be bothered with on its own. In fact, I'm kind of glad that someone is doing our job for us. The more concerning thing is that we've received intelligence that a new crime boss is moving to town. We believe that this new player is going to make a move to run the criminal organization in much of the western world."

Appleton paused for dramatic effect before continuing. "Few people can pull this off under the radar. To do so, you need a global network, business fronts to clean your money, and massive legitimate and illegitimate influence to discreetly push things through."

Appleton stopped and flashed up a photo of one man. He looked tall, fit, and lean. The image showed him walking in a suit with sunglasses and talking on the phone. This was clearly a surveillance photo, pulled from a file probably filled with other information. Next to that picture, a second photograph appeared on the screen, a close-up of just the man's face. The man appeared to be in his late thirties, with intelligent eyes, ebony skin, and oddly enough, a big charming smile. The picture looked like it belonged on a professional bio, not a case file.

"We received a tip that this is our guy." Appleton finished his grand reveal.

"Who is that?" asked Cramer.

"Someone who flies completely under the radar," Appleton replied. "This is Ori Clayborn, Founder, and CEO of the Singularity Group."

Chapter 8

Evelyn remained quiet, observing the group, ready to take in the new information.

Deputy Director Chisholm said, "Special Agent Chivington, tell us what you have."

Chivington began to go through his file. "Many people don't know Ori Clayborn's background. He seems to be a rags-to-riches story of sorts."

The big screen split, one-half still showed Ori's picture, while a list of details populated on the other half of the screen.

"His parents split up when he was young. He was raised by his mother in a single-family home. We pulled school records, and it looks like he was a smart kid. However, he left school at sixteen and fell off the grid. Then about ten years ago, he popped back up as the CEO and Founder of the Singularity Group."

"What do we know about his mother?" Section Chief Appleton asked.

"She only has a high school education but somehow runs the IT department for a network of medical professionals," Chivington said.

"What do we know about the Singularity Group?" Section Chief Appleton asked.

"It's privately held, so it's hard to truly get an understanding of its value, but our best estimates are that the company is worth billions," Chivington said.

"What does the company do?" Special Agent Cramer asked.

"They are involved in several different business endeavors, like a private conglomerate," Mikiko said. "Singularity Group first got noticed for developing software that allows small businesses to buy goods and supplies at the same price as major retail companies, increasing the competitive advantage of the small business owner. Then it implemented a successful micro-financing type of business model in underserved communities in the US. It also has stakes in companies across an array of industries."

Everyone looked at Mikiko with surprise. She shrugged and said, "I watch documentaries."

"So, we have a high school dropout who goes missing and then comes back as the head of a company worth billions of dollars?" Deputy Director Chisholm asked. "How is that possible?"

"It's hard for me to believe that he did all this by providing banking services in the ghettos," Appleton added. "There's no money there."

"That's one way of looking at it," Evelyn said. "Or perhaps he found a way to provide financial solutions to the eighty-eight million or twenty-eight percent of the US population who were not receiving any insured banking solutions, thus crippling the predatory lending or payday cash industry," Evelyn stated.

It was Evelyn's turn to get stared at. She shrugged and said, "I like documentaries too."

Appleton glared at Evelyn, "It's more than that, though, isn't it, Agent Blackwood? Do you want to enlighten us?"

Evelyn didn't even acknowledge Appleton's question, still staring at the photo on the screen.

"But it doesn't sound like he became a billionaire serving this community alone," Cramer noted.

Special Agent Chivington continued, "True. After establishing relationships in the different communities, his company started to provide consulting services to the businesses that they offered loans to, in exchange for a percentage of the businesses' earnings. In several instances, they acquired small parts of the businesses to have more say in the day-to-day operations, pretty much becoming a private equity firm of sorts. They were then able to deploy the software that Agent Shikibu mentioned. It syncs all of the businesses in their network so that when Sam's family-run shop in Athens, Tennessee, orders more toilet paper or batteries, they get the same price as your big-box stores and giant online retailers."

"So, he's helping grow the middle class? He sounds truly dangerous," Agent Shikibu whispered with sarcasm.

"Talk about his criminal program," said Appleton vehemently.

"The most controversial of his endeavors is the Criminal Relief Work Program. This initiative places formerly incarcerated people in jobs within and throughout his many companies. He calls it Project Legacy."

Cramer asked, "So he's using cheap labor across his companies?"

"He's not treating them as cheap labor. We were able to get our hands on records that show he pays them competitive wages and benefits, and he even provides them with counseling," an analyst added before Appleton shot him a look that clearly said his voice was not welcome.

"Why would he do that?" Cramer asked.

"That's a great question," said Appleton.

"That's one of the main reasons we think that he could be our guy. With his access to and ownership of a vast array of businesses that could act as fronts, plus his convict program, we believe he's been able to set up a strong, diverse network of criminal affiliates. And most importantly, his entire business is run as a private company, so no one knows who he is or what he's doing," said Chivington.

"Discretion," Evelyn said in a low tone.

Appleton jumped back in. "This guy is worth billions, and most people have never even heard of him. As I mentioned earlier, I have heard from a reliable source that he is our guy. We are setting up a special task force to bust his ass and take down his entire organization."

"Who's this source? And what proof do they have? This all sounds highly speculative," Evelyn said.

With a scornful look, Appleton responded, "Agent Blackwood, that information is above your pay grade. The case against him is quite clear."

"Because he gives jobs to people who served time in jail? I need actual evidence and not hearsay." Evelyn paused and collected herself. "Look, I remember this kid from grade school. He was brilliant, maybe a genius. He was stubborn, but principled and kind. I remember thinking that this kid was going to be the president one day. He was that kind of guy. So I am in no way surprised that he's very successful. I am, however, having a hard time wrapping my head around this narrative." She took a deep breath, and continued, "Why am I here?"

Appleton smiled. "I'm glad you finally asked, Agent Blackwood. When Agent Chivington was researching our suspect, we did notice that you and our suspect had some overlapping time at school. Were you friends?"

"We were in a lot of the same classes," Evelyn replied coolly.

"We want you, as a friendly face, to talk to Clayborn," Deputy Director Chisholm said.

"I'm not sure how much help I can provide. I mean, it's been years since I've seen the guy. His files say it; he left school early," Evelyn said.

The deputy director continued, "We know that he is a very private man, but hopefully he will open up to a familiar face. Think of it like this; if he's innocent, then there's nothing to worry about."

Then Appleton weighed in, "But we don't think that's the case. Our source has tipped us off that a deal is going down where we can finally nail him and his criminal enterprise. We're talking money laundering on a massive scale, connections with La Tiniebla Cartel, and who knows what else."

"You and your team are known for analyzing data patterns to find the evidence and trends that everyone else misses," Deputy Director Chisholm said. "Besides your connection to Clayborn, your ability to uncover the truth is another reason why I specifically asked Section Chief Appleton to add you to this assignment. You are the best mind we have."

Several phones started buzzing. Mikiko quickly left the room to take a call.

"If I'm going to work this, I insist on having Agent Shikibu with me as well," Evelyn said.

"Of course, that's why she's here too," the deputy director said. "You two have been pretty much attached at the hip since the academy."

Mikiko bursts back in the room, looking at the deputy director with a concerned expression. "There was an explosion today," she shared.

"Where?" Evelyn asked.

"At the corporate headquarters of the Singularity Group," Mikiko replied.

Evelyn took a deep breath. "Any casualties?"

"We aren't sure yet, but there's a team on the ground en route now," Mikiko responded.

Deputy Director Chisolm looked at Evelyn. "We will have a plane ready in thirty minutes to get you to Atlanta. You can be there within a couple of hours."

Appleton took the opportunity to chime in, "You will be taking Special Agent Chivington and Cramer with you to provide backup. This car bomb could be the start of a war."

As Evelyn turned to leave, Appleton called after her, "What do you say now, Agent Blackwood? Still don't think he's connected to the cartel?"

Chapter 9

"Jefe," the young man said. "El embajador está aquí para verlo."

The ambassador of which *country is here to see me,* Carlos thought to himself. "Gracias, chico."

The ambassador walked in, and Carlos greeted him, "Señor embajador, mucho gusto."

"It is nice to meet you as well, Don Carlos," the ambassador said. "Do you mind if we speak in English? I would appreciate a little privacy."

"Oh, of course, I do not mind," Carlos said. "Would you like a drink?"

"Yes, please," the ambassador nodded.

Carlos goes behind the bar and pours the añejo aged tequila, neat, in the two beautiful crystal brandy snifters. Carlos slides the short stem of the brandy snifter between his middle and ring finger, cupping the cool crystal ball glass in the palm of his hand. He hands the other snifter to the ambassador. "Please, let's step outside and enjoy this beautiful weather," Carlos said.

Once outside, Carlos began, "So, what brings you to my door, Mr. Ambassador?"

"Straight to business then," the ambassador said with a hint of discomfort.

"Unfortunately, there have been some recent events that are occupying a lot of my attention, which leaves me with a minimal amount of time for . . .," Carlos paused for the right words, "other pursuits."

"I see. Well, I'm sure that you are well aware of the problem my country is facing with gang violence. It has gotten out of control, and there's nothing that we can do to stop it. We don't have the resources because we can't stabilize our economy and because people are too afraid to go to work. We cannot rely on tourism because everyone is afraid of getting kidnapped for ransom. We quite frankly do not have the resources to deal with this issue ourselves."

"What about the Americans or the Europeans?" Carlos asked.

"You know how the Americans are. They are mainly focused on keeping the violence out of their borders even though these gangs started in their prisons and they deported these violent monsters to our country," the ambassador said. "The Europeans show little interest in our problems as well."

"What is it that you want from me, Mr. Ambassador?" Carlos said as he gazed off in the distance. The view from Carlos's estate looked over a vast valley, plush with perfectly aligned rows of agave. There were workers in each row, delicately trimming and pruning the plants.

"We—" the ambassador started.

Carlos quickly interrupted him, "We who?"

"My government sent me here to see if you would be willing to help us," the ambassador said.

"Help you slay your monsters?" Carlos asked.

"Sí," the Ambassador said.

"What makes you think that I would be willing to do that?" Carlos asked.

"We could make it worth your while," the ambassador said. "You are a businessman, correct? I'm sure that we can come up with some agreement."

"What type of agreement did you have in mind?" Carlos asked.

"To begin, we could turn a blind eye to any business interests you may have in our country and free up transportation routes," the ambassador said.

Carlos didn't respond and kept his gaze on the valley.

"We will also guarantee full immunity to anyone in your organization, as long as you end the violence," the ambassador said.

Carlos then focused his stare on a worker far away in the valley. "Mr. Ambassador, what makes you think that I am the right person to take care of this gang problem for you?"

"I'm very aware of your reputation. You are one of the most feared men in the world," the ambassador said.

"Honestly, Don Carlos, we have heard stories of your methods, and they are clearly effective. Everyone who knows who you are, fears you."

"Do you know why I do it? Why I've done the things that I've done?" Carlos asked.

"You are your only competition. You control the market." The ambassador suggested, "To successfully become the market leader. To become one of the wealthiest people in history."

Carlos, with a grin on his face, stared directly into the ambassador's eyes. "So you think I've done everything you've heard I've done for money?" The smile slowly melted away from his face while he still locked eyes with his visitor. The ambassador attempted to divert his eyes to look elsewhere. "Is that all you think of me?" Carlos asked.

Carlos looked back at the person working in the field and gave the ambassador a moment to consider.

"We've heard a rumor that you had something to do with reducing America's opioid epidemic," the ambassador finally said.

"It sounds like there is a lot of gossip around my business arrangements," Carlos said. "Can I assume you know what happens if you betray me?"

"I can imagine what would happen," the ambassador said.

"Let's take a walk; I think better when I walk." As they walked through Carlos's estate, he said, "You know, I have a vision. Contrary to what many people think, I do what I do because I like to offer people an opportunity to live a good life. Do you see that man working in the field?" Carlos pointed to the worker that he was staring at earlier. "I'm sure that you remember that there was a time in my country when violence and murder ran rampant. No one could control it, and people were starving and scared. So, I decided to do something about it. I needed to be extremely ruthless to take the reins of the truly wild beast that is greed and corruption. I had a vision: do whatever I have to do to eradicate what I think is the true monster. I believe that an honest, good person should have the chance to live a good life. But I realized that for people to have that, someone needed to step up and allow that to happen."

Carlos took a sniff of the tequila, still not taking a sip from the glass. "For me to partner with others, I require that they are one hundred percent committed to my vision. A world where freedom to pursue dreams exists for all those who are good people."

"We can most definitely be aligned to your vision," the ambassador said.

"I require more than *aligning* to my vision," Carlos said. "Your vision will need to be my vision. I'll accept nothing less. And before you respond, I need you to understand — this is a solemn commitment, and you need to understand the repercussions of betraying me. Without a vision, you will be lost wandering around in the darkness. Do you understand, Ambassador?"

"I believe I do," the ambassador replied quickly.

"When you landed your private jet at my airport, and you traveled with your security guards to my home, tell me, how did you feel?" Carlos asked.

"I— I felt—," the Ambassador stammered. "I felt safe."

"Do you know why that is?" Carlos asked.

"You have crime under control here?"

"Yes, that is correct. But that didn't just happen, Mr. Ambassador. It's become this way because I am a very demanding person. Crime is not just at an all-time low in this region, but it's also low in any region where I have operations. For being a part of my vision, I offer people peace and prosperity." Carlos paused. "Any endeavor I pursue must be about the vision, not about stomping out a problem. There is much good that could be done in your country, but it must start with the right purpose. Besides, the gangs in your country do keep the Western government and media very busy. Removing them from the equation will give the Westerners more time to turn their focus onto . . ." Carlos paused before continuing, "other groups that they deem a possible threat."

"Innocent, good people are scared to leave their homes. They live in fear," the ambassador said.

"I understand, and I truly do feel sorry for them," Carlos said. "You are the elected officials tasked with protecting the people. What actions are you taking?"

The ambassador started to speak, but Carlos cut him off.

"I don't think I want to hear your excuses about how you've tried everything and nothing works." Carlos looked at the ambassador. "If you are honest with yourself, you will accept that it's a complicated problem to solve and you and your peers don't feel like getting your hands that dirty." Carlos continued, "Have you ever thought about why these gangs continue to grow and be a problem?"

"These gangs force people to cooperate. The numbers are growing out of fear," the ambassador said.

"How is it that the citizens of your country feel like they have no other option? It's your job to protect your citizens, and you and your people are failing. That's your one job, to protect your citizens. So, if you aren't protecting your citizens, then who are you protecting?" Carlos said.

"Well," the ambassador started to speak.

"That was rhetorical. I know who you are protecting; it's yourself. The most elite and wealthiest of you could solve this problem, but you choose not to. So, you come to me, fully knowing who and what I am, and you ask me to solve this problem that you all chose not to solve."

"Does this mean that you will not help us?" the ambassador said.

"Not necessarily," Carlos said. "I just went on that little rant to remind you that this is a conscious choice that you are making. You and your peers can resolve this on your own and are choosing to come to me. Fortunately for you, there are things that I could use that you and your government can provide. It could be worth me intervening."

Carlos cleared his throat, quickly wrapped his hand around the back of the ambassador's neck, and forced the ambassador's face inches away from his. The ambassador's guards reached for their pistols, and instantly, two dozen of Carlos's guards and employees drew their firearms and pointed them toward the ambassador and his guards. The ambassador slowly waved at his guards, using his hand to instruct them to lower their weapons.

Carlos smiled, inches from the ambassador's face. "Listen to me very, very carefully. If you decide to ever, ever betray me, you will receive a punishment infinitely worse than death. You will wander in darkness until the day I allow you to stop breathing. Do you understand?"

The ambassador nodded his head timidly.

"I need to hear you say it. Do. You. Understand?" Carlos said slowly, with a smile on his face.

"I— I understand."

"Excellent!" Carlos said with a jovial tone as he let the ambassador go. All of Carlos's people holstered their weapons.

"There are three other things that I need from you in exchange for my services," Carlos said. "Sugar is one of your country's largest exports. I need to diversify my business portfolio and have been interested in getting into the sugar business."

"I think that we can figure something out," the ambassador said.

"Good. For the second thing," Carlos continued, "I have some people who are great candidates for high-level cabinet positions within your government, with access to the information that I need. I would appreciate your support and discretion to sponsor them and ensure that they obtain the appropriate positions."

"What positions specifically?" the ambassador asked.

"It doesn't matter; this is non-negotiable. Lastly, I need you to fully understand what will happen if you want me to help clean up your problem." Carlos paused, then continued. "But tell me this, how long after I rid your country of its gang problem until you and your western friends turn their attention onto me?"

"Why would we ever come after you? If you help us with our problem, then we would see you as an ally," the ambassador said.

"Whose allegiance do you value more, mine or that of the US Government?" Carlos asked.

"I . . . I . . . mean," the ambassador stammers.

"You know what's interesting?" Carlos said with a smile. "I hate this business, I hate it. Now don't get me wrong, I love the money and all the things that I can buy with it. But you know what, if people bought bananas as much as they buy some of my other products, I'd be the king of bananas. The point is, there's a market for what I provide. This poison. The people who use this type of poison know exactly what it is. If you do too much, it will kill you. Yet they feel like this escape from reality, from their reality, is worth the risk."

"These governments look at me like I'm the problem when I'm just the escape from the reality that they've created," Carlos said as he looked around at the fields.

Chapter 10

Agents from the Georgia Bureau of Investigation, or the GBI as they are referred to, and the FBI agents are all over the corporate parking lot, collecting an assortment of charred car parts. After combing through the debris from the explosion, one of the GBI agents yelled out, "I found something."

Evelyn glanced over as his superior shouted, "What do you have?"

"It's nothing extremely sophisticated," he said as he used a pen to move around the different components of the bomb. Evelyn and Special Agent Chivington moved closer to examine the heap of burned metal and melted plastic. "The bomber used C-4 connected to a timer and a trigger that could be set off remotely."

"Why would they have a timer and a remote trigger?" asked the agent in charge.

The GBI bomb specialist said, "I don't think that the bomber was an expert with explosives. A professional would be using something more sophisticated. This is sloppy work for a high-profile target," the bomb specialist said.

"Maybe someone wanted to send a message. It's a pretty common explosive found in vendettas between crime families," Cramer offered as he walked closer to a group of people gathered around the debris.

"And what message might that be?" Evelyn asked.

Cramer shrugged and said, "Well, that's the question we are here to figure out, right?"

Evelyn raised an eyebrow and turned back to the evidence. "I think all it tells us so far is that someone wanted flexibility. What time did the witnesses say that the bomb went off?"

"Around twelve-fifteen pm," the GBI agent said. "I guess whoever planted this explosive device wanted to set it off while the driver was on his way to lunch. It appears as though it went off via remote trigger, not the timer, though."

Evelyn looked up and noticed the cameras on the light posts in the parking lot and the cameras in the front entrance that pointed directly to the parked car. "Maybe they were watching the car and knew when to push the button." Evelyn shifted her attention, "Hey, Mikiko?"

"Yeah," Mikiko said as she walked over to Evelyn.

"Let's pull all the video feeds from these cameras. Let's also pull the video from every camera that has an angle on this car for the past month."

"Got it. Do you think we need to pull the video feed from Clayborn's house too?" Mikiko asked.

"Please comb through any camera footage you can get your hands on." Evelyn held a piece of the detonator closer to her eyes. "I don't think this has been on this car longer than a couple of weeks. Maybe we will get lucky. I would imagine that he goes to work and goes home and puts his car in a garage. He most likely takes the same route every day, so let's see if we can find out all the stops he's made, and maybe we can find out when this was put on his car."

"Let me go ask Clayborn about video from his home," said Mikiko as she turned to walk into the building.

"Why do you think this device was planted on the car within the last couple of weeks?" Chivington asked.

"The bomb was placed under the car, and there's a sticker on the windshield that shows the last oil change was two weeks ago. The people who replaced the oil would've noticed some strange device on the car. So, either the people who changed his oil planted this device, or the device was planted after the car received maintenance."

"We've been seeing some people taking on contract work for the cartel. Real sloppy work," the GBI agent said, shaking his head. "This was mainly in the outskirts of town. A lot of people who were cooking and dealing crystal meth were getting pushed out."

"I read some reports on that." Evelyn said. "Were you boys ever able to tie any of the deaths directly to the cartel?"

"No, ma'am," the agent said, starting to become defensive. "We knew for a fact it was them. They just always somehow . . ."

"I get it." Evelyn sympathized. "That's the worst when you know who it is, but they just always slip through your fingers. I read the witness statements from friends and family members of the cartel's targets. Every single one of them said that a member of the cartel always visited the victim within a week of the hit to offer them the chance to reconsider declining the offer."

"That's right," the GBI agent nodded. "And it was the damnedest thing. There were some guys, hell, families even, who were big in the meth game. Suddenly, they went cold turkey. We always assumed that they got the same warning from the cartel, but no one would ever speak about it."

That sparked a thought, and Evelyn walked quickly to the front lobby, "Where are you going?" Chivington yelled after her.

Evelyn didn't answer and walked to the security officer in the lobby. "I need the visitor list for the past two weeks."

"What are you looking for?" Cramer appeared by her side.

Evelyn took the book, still looking at the security guard at the front desk. "I'll also need to have the footage from every camera that has an angle of this book as well as the data to show who badged in and when."

"Are you thinking that the bomber visited Clayborn before today to give him a chance to reconsider?" Chivington asked.

"Not necessarily the bomber, but some representative from the cartel," Evelyn said. "We should be able to cross-reference the badge data with the sign-in details, facial recognition, and professional networking websites to see if there was anyone meeting with Clayborn or anyone in the company who shouldn't be here."

"Do you think that the cartel would have made themselves visible here before attempting to blow up Clayborn's car?" Agent Cramer asked sarcastically.

"It was you who said that someone could have been sending Clayborn a message," Evelyn said. "If your theory is right, and you think that he has ties to the cartel, then this will strengthen the case."

"Do we know how the victims are?" Evelyn asked.

"No casualties, some scrapes and bruises, but they should be getting out of the on-site clinic by now," Chivington said.

"Let's get down what they remember and see if they have any idea of who would want to do this or why," Evelyn said.

Just then the elevator opened, and Mikiko joined them again. "Evelyn!" she said.

"What do you have, Mikiko?" Evelyn asked.

"The device had to have been installed right here in the parking lot."

"Why is that?" Evelyn asked.

Mikiko continued, "Because if the bomber had followed this car, they would have learned that Clayborn doesn't drive this vehicle. So, the culprits either wanted to kill the main security guard, which makes no sense, or they installed the bomb here."

Chapter 11

Evelyn knocked twice on Roger Garrison's door. "Mr. Garrison, are you feeling up to answering a few questions?"

"Sure, please come in," Roger said while Agents Chivington, Cramer, and Blackwood entered his office and pulled up seats to get closer to Roger's glass desk.

"How long have you known Mr. Clayborn?" Cramer asked.

"Ori and I met probably fifteen years ago while I was studying to get my MBA. This young-looking guy came to my MBA program looking for an intern to help stand up one of his early business ideas. I was looking to do something different, so I figured, why not," Roger said, shrugging his shoulders.

"Ori needed someone with financial and accounting knowledge who would also act as the devil's advocate and challenge his views. He thought that I would be a good addition to his company."

"Did you and Mr. Clayborn ever argue over anything?" Chivington asked.

"We were constantly debating, over almost everything," Roger said. "But, that's part of the reason he brought me in. He liked my difference of opinion."

"What are some of the things you've fought over?" Cramer said.

"Debated," Roger replied swiftly.

"Excuse me?" Cramer said.

"You meant to ask me about some of the things we've debated. We never fought." Roger continued, "One constant debate was if we should take the company public."

"What was the source of the debate?" Chivington asked.

"Ori never wanted to sell shares of this company on the public market," Roger said. "I, of course, was all about it. I would argue that if we had more capital, then we would be able to expand so much faster. But Ori wasn't interested."

"Why not?" Evelyn asked.

"He would always say that he doesn't want to turn over control of his firm to the short-term vision of shareholders."

"Your business model seems successful. Do you know how Mr. Clayborn is doing financially? Is there any indication that he is having any trouble with money? Does everything seem good with the accounting?" Cramer asked.

Roger responded sharply, "There was absolutely nothing strange with our books. To ensure that there's no fraud or theft of any kind, Ori put a process in place where our accountant, whose name is Warren, Ori, and I each review the financials in individual meetings with the external independent accounting and audit firms." Roger continued, his eyes locked on Agent Cramer, "What are you implying?"

"I'm not implying anything; I'm trying to understand why someone would want to place a bomb on Mr. Clayborn's car," Cramer said. "It would not be the first time that we find someone who got into financial trouble and made a deal with the wrong people."

"That's not like Ori. If he had any financial issues, then I would have known," Roger said, still visibly angry with the line of questioning.

"How would you know?" Evelyn asked.

"If Ori needed the money, he would have started to deposit his paycheck into his personal bank account, as opposed to the employee bonus pool," Roger said.

"What do you mean?" Agent Chivington asked.

"Ori never really collects a paycheck. I mean," Roger paused, "he did get a paycheck from here, but he would donate the majority of it back to a savings account to pay out all employee bonuses at the end of the year." Roger turned to look out of the window and went quiet. The agents realized that he started to tear up as he turned back, his eyes red. "I honestly don't know who would try to hurt Ori. This company, and all it does . . . I don't think he does any of it for himself. He seems more concerned with making sure that everyone else is all right."

The door to Roger's office slowly cracked open, and Mikiko's face peeked from behind it. "Agent Blackwood, Ms. Leslie Ochoa is ready to speak."

Evelyn turned back to Roger. "Thank you for speaking with us. We'll follow up with you if we have more questions. Get some rest if you can."

Chapter 12

Evelyn, Agent Chivington, and Agent Cramer all walked over to greet Leslie in front of her office.

"Do you mind if we speak in the conference room?" Leslie asked.

"Wherever you feel most comfortable," Evelyn responded.

"We are truly sorry for what's happened here, and we will get to the bottom of this," Cramer said.

"I still don't understand why anyone would do . . ." Leslie started to say as she teared up and crossed her arms to hug her own shoulders.

"Don't worry; you are safe," Evelyn said, making eye contact with Leslie. Evelyn walked over to the wall, pressed her finger against it, and said, "Privacy, please."

She looked back at Leslie, "We will do everything in our power to make sure that the people behind this are brought to justice."

Leslie took a deep breath, tucked her hair behind her ears, and placed her hands on her legs. "Let me know how I can help."

Agent Chivington jumped in. "Do you know if there's anyone who would be after Mr. Clayborn?"

"After Ori?" Leslie asked in disbelief. "Not at all. Everyone loves Ori."

"That's what we hear. But we are having a hard time trying to understand why something like this would happen to a man that is so highly regarded," Cramer said.

"Has anything out of the ordinary happened lately? Has Mr. Clayborn been behaving differently?" Chivington asked.

"No, Ori has been positive and relaxed as usual." Leslie thought for a minute. "Do you think this has something to do with Tony?"

"Tony? Who's Tony?" Cramer asked.

"He does private investigative research for the company, right?" Evelyn asked.

"Yes, and we haven't heard from him in a couple of days," Leslie said.

"When did you last see him?" Cramer asked.

"That's hard to say," Leslie said. "It was maybe a few months ago. I usually only see him when he has information that needs to be delivered in person."

"How do you communicate with him?" Cramer asked.

"We can call him or send him a text message, and he always responds. That was until this past week." Leslie got a panicked expression. "Oh my God! Do you think something could have happened to him too?"

"We aren't sure. We haven't heard anything about Tony, but my partner, Agent Shikibu, will look into it," Evelyn said.

"How long have you known Tony?" Chivington asked.

"Several years now. We met when I was still working at my law firm. I was looking for someone who could conduct private investigations for some of my more challenging cases. Tony happened to be looking for additional work at the time, and Ori introduced us. Ori told me that he and Tony go way back and that he's a good guy. He's rough around the edges, but he is reliable and has a good heart. So, I used him for a few cases, and he did great work. Tony operates alone and with discretion. He always delivers and never does anything compromising. I can't imagine that he would be involved in anything like this."

"So, you can't think of anyone who would have it out for your boss?" Cramer asked.

"No, I can't," Leslie said.

"Okay, thank you for your time," Chivington said as he stood up to signal that she could leave.

"One last question," Evelyn said. "What was the last thing that Tony was researching for you?"

Chapter 13

"Excuse me," Agent Chivington said as he knocks on Ori's office door.

"Oh, yes, please come in."

"Is now still an appropriate time for you to meet with us?" Evelyn asked. "How are you feeling?"

"Of course, we should talk now while everything is still fresh in my memory. If you don't mind, I'd like Jordan and Leslie to stay," Ori said, gesturing over to the other side of the room where they were sitting.

"It's your call," Cramer said with an annoyed tone. The other agents simultaneous sent him a sharp glare.

Ori, in response, quickly became less pleasant. "How may I help you, Agent— What was your name again?" Ori locked his stare on Cramer.

Chivington stepped forward and extended his hand. "I'm Agent Chivington, this is Agent Blackwood, and our very rude colleague there is Agent Cramer. We are with the Federal Bureau of Investigation and are here to find out who is behind this attack."

"We have a few questions that we hope you can help us answer," Evelyn said in a warm tone.

"Sure, Agent Blackwood, how can I be of service?" Ori replied with a smile spreading across his face, until he suddenly grimaced and grabbed his head. Jordan quickly moved toward his side to aid him. Ori quickly extended his hand, signaling her to stop. Jordan was small in stature, but her calm and resolve commanded attention.

"It's just a slight headache. It will be fine in a matter of time." He smiled again. "Please, what questions do you have for me?"

"I know you've been through a lot, but can you help us understand who would have done this?" Evelyn asked. "Does anyone have it out for you?"

"I've been trying to think of who would want to do something like this, and I am drawing a blank," Ori said.

"Do you have any enemies or anyone that may have issues with you?" Chivington asked.

"Not that I'm aware of. I mean, any business deal I get involved in, if we don't all walk away feeling good about the relationship, then it's not a deal for us. We have regular meetings with all of our business partners, and we don't have any reason to believe that anyone is unhappy, especially unhappy enough to do something like this."

"What about any business deal that you walked away from? Do you think someone is harboring any resentment?" Chivington asked.

"No, not that I can think of," Ori said.

"What about your employees, do you think any of them could have wanted to harm you?" Evelyn asked.

"No, I can't imagine any one of them trying to do this. Our employee satisfaction is a critical part of our company's success. If any of our employees have a grievance, we have several forums for them to share their concerns. I'm very accessible to all of them if they need me."

"Is it true that you don't have a salary?" Cramer asked.

"No," Ori replied without looking in Cramer's direction.

"No, you don't have a salary?" Cramer responded sharply.

Ori looked over and saw that the agent was glaring at him. He smiled and shifted his entire body to face Agent Cramer. "No, Agent, it is not true that I don't have a salary. I, in fact, do have a salary. I just choose not to take it. I donate most of it to the employees."

Agent Cramer said with a sly smile, "Can you tell us how a man who lives the lifestyle that you live cannot take a salary? How do you fund your lavish lifestyle?"

"What Agent Cramer is trying to say," Evelyn interceded, softening the message, "is do you have other sources of income not tied to this company that could have made someone upset? Maybe a business venture that you are not as actively involved in?"

"No, Agent Blackwood, I make it a point to be somewhat involved in all of my endeavors." He looked back at Agent Cramer. "And to answer your question, I've done incredibly well with some of my earlier ventures, which has allowed me to not need to take compensation from this place."

"Then why do you even have a salary?" Chivington asked.

"Oh, that's not for me, that's for my replacement. Whoever that will be. As I am sure you are aware, we have been a remarkably successful company, and I won't be here forever. A precedent needed to be set regarding how much the CEO of this company should make."

"And why is that?" Cramer asked.

"Someone has to repair the breach," Ori said under his breath, but just loud enough for the agents to hear him.

"What does that mean?" Cramer asked.

"Listen, we are trying to understand what is going on here and why this happened to you at your business," Chivington asked. "Do the words Tiniebla Cartel sound familiar to you, Mr. Clayborn?"

"I've heard of them before," Ori said.

"What do you know about them?" Chivington continued.

"I read somewhere that the government suspects that this group is the cartel of all cartels."

"That's it? That's all you know about them?" Cramer asked.

"What are you talking about?" Ori said.

"Don't play coy," Cramer said. "It's only a matter of time before we find enough evidence of your connection with the cartel. You've upset them somehow and are now on the outs. If you start talking now, then we can protect you."

"You clearly have an angle here, Agent Cramer," Leslie chimed in. "I think that Ori is done speaking with you now."

"Do you know anything about this cartel?" Chivington asked. "Your silence right now isn't making you look very innocent. If you are somehow connected to them, speak now. Only guilty people don't cooperate."

"You would hope that's the case, wouldn't you, Agent Chivington?" Ori said as he pulled out his phone. "Sorry, one moment please."

Chapter 14

"Be wary of the web."

Ori's thumbs moved quickly as he responded to the text message that he received, "Who is this, and how did you get this number?"

The mysterious text messenger replied, "You've had the same number for a very long time. You know all too well the importance of trusting your intuition. It's one of the universe's preferred communication methods. You are being set up. Why would they be so quick to try and put you into protective custody? If you go with them, your life as you know it will be over."

"Excuse me, Mr. Clayborn. We are trying to find out who tried to blow you up. Is that something that can wait?" Cramer asked.

Ori looked up and saw that everyone around the room had shifted their focus onto him sending a message on his phone. "I'm sorry. This is just a dear friend checking in on me. Just give me one minute."

Leslie said again, "Like I said, we are all done here."

Ori tucked his phone back in his jacket pocket and looked around the room. "Jordan?"

"I'm here." Jordan appeared from behind the three agents.

"How are the others?" Ori asked.

"Roger and Hetty are still fine. You were the closest one to the car, so we probably need to get you to the hospital," Jordan said.

"I'm fine, I don't need to go to the hospital," Ori said.

"You need to see a doctor," Jordan said.

Agent Blackwood joined in, "You need a doctor and some rest. We have a few more questions for you later, but for now, we need to get you better and to make sure that you are safe." She turned to Jordan, "Is there a physician on site?"

"We have a physician's assistant on staff," Jordan replied.

"Sir, why don't you have the physician's assistant come up here to check you out and make sure you are okay, then we will continue with our questions later," Agent Blackwood suggests. "Jordan, please call the physician's assistant and have her come to Ori's office. We will give you some privacy," she added, and Jordan nodded, turning to leave the office.

Leslie looked puzzled. That was the first time that she had ever seen Jordan listen to anyone other than Ori himself.

"I recognize you," Ori said.

"Yes," Agent Blackwood said. "We were in grade school together."

"Evelyn, right?" Ori said, leaning back in his seat, finally relaxing.

"Yes, but it's Agent Blackwood for now. We will speak again soon," Evelyn said and turned to leave his office.

Ori pulled back out his phone to review another message from the unknown number. There were a limited number of people who had this mobile number and they were instructed to never allow anyone else access. If this unknown messenger was who Ori thought it was, then something was seriously wrong. They all decided only to use this phone in extreme emergencies.

Ori looked back down at his phone to review the new message from the unknown number, which read, "It's time. I sincerely wish you the best of luck."

As the other agents began to leave the office, Agent Chivington started to speak, "Mr. Clayborn, we don't think that it's safe for you right now. We believe that some ruthless people may be after you. I'm going to recommend that we put you in protective custody."

"Wait, what are you talking about? What ruthless people? And you want him to go into protective custody when? Now?" Leslie rattled off questions, quickly becoming tense.

Ori remained calm and collected, not showing nearly as much emotion.

"Do you know who did this?" Leslie asked the agents.

"It's too early to say. We have a few early theories, but we need to collect more evidence to be sure. But we do need to go right now," Chivington said.

Ori feels the vibration in his hand from his phone buzzing from a new message. He glances down and reads, "You need to get out of there now. You are in more danger than you know. Bring your lawyer friend too; she's also at risk."

He received another message, "You and the lawyer need to get out of that room and that building now! Be outside in five minutes."

Jordan entered the office again. "The physician's assistant is on her way up. What's going on? I feel the tension in the air."

"These agents think that Ori needs to go into protective custody," Leslie said.

"This is a lot to process," Ori started. "Let me see the physician's assistant first; then we will continue this conversation. Does that sound good, Agent Chivington?"

"That sounds good for now," Chivington said as he left the room.

Only Ori, Jordan, and Leslie were left in the office. Ori looked to Jordan. "Something is not right."

"I agree," Jordan said.

"Leslie and I need to go. You know what to do," Ori told her.

Jordan merely nodded and left the office, closing the door behind her.

Chapter 15

As soon as Leslie and Ori were alone in the office, Ori said, "I know that this is going to sound strange, but you've got to trust me. Something does not feel right about these FBI agents and protective custody."

"I absolutely agree. I can't put my finger on it, but something just doesn't pass the sniff test." Leslie said, and she becomes concerned.

"I can't explain right now, but we've got to get out of here. Those text messages that I received were from someone trying to warn me that we can't trust these agents," he said. "And I'm concerned that there's a connection with Tony's absence."

"Who was it?" She asked.

"I . . ." Ori hesitated. "It's someone who has never lied to me before. We need to get out of here now, and no one can see us leave."

"Well, how on Earth do you propose we do that?" Leslie asked.

Ori walked toward the far wall in his office. As he got closer, a door revealed itself. Once Ori was a foot away from the door, it slid open, and to Leslie's surprise, it was a bathroom. Ori turned back to her and said, "Are you coming?"

The tile covering the floors and walls was a beautiful black marble, but the veins in the stone were vibrant pinks, yellows, and greens. The veins seemed to be moving and flowing, like a river. Leslie had a strange feeling in the bathroom, like the walls were alive. Leslie noticed that there were no light fixtures in the bathroom. All the lights were radiating from the veins in the tile.

"What is this?" she asked Ori.

"It's just a bathroom," Ori said with a smile. "And this is a toilet," Ori closed the toilet seat lid. "Going down, please." Suddenly, a wall opened, and Leslie was surprised to see an elevator.

As they got in, Leslie noticed that there were only two buttons, one clearly to get to his office. She asked, "Where does this go?"

"It goes directly to Ms. Hetty's office," he said. "A few years ago, when they were doing major renovations on the floor, I asked a security team to come in and build this for me."

"Who has access to use this?" she asked without really knowing why. And why or how would he anticipate anyone feeling the need to get away in such a discreet manner?

"Well, just me, Jordan, and you, actually," he said. "Although I never made you aware, I figured I'd set you up with access just in case of an emergency. Also, Ms. Hetty has access. She enjoys having a private bathroom."

As the door opened, they appeared to be in some faux storage closet. Ori continued moving forward as the door closed behind them. Leslie noticed that the door was cleverly disguised as a wall with storage shelves on it.

"Why would you even need something like this?" Leslie started asking.

"Not now, I'll tell you later. Right now, we've got to keep moving," he said as they walked out of the storage closet. They entered Ms. Hetty's private office. They checked her monitors and saw that only Ms. Hetty was in the security break room.

Surprised to see Leslie, Ms. Hetty quickly said, "What's wrong? Did something else happen?"

"Not exactly. But something is off, and we need to get out of here," Ori replied.

"Well, you know I've got your back. Go through the service entrance to the parking garage," she said without hesitation. "Gus and Al should be there."

As they walked toward the back exit to the parking deck, they saw an FBI agent patrolling that exit and more agents surveying the area near the explosion. Ori and

Leslie stayed out of sight. Ori and Leslie paused as they tried to figure out the next step. Leslie's breath quickened. Then she saw Ori lock eyes with one the custodians, Gus, who signaled the two to follow him. They waited a beat and then started moving toward him. As they did, one of the other custodians, Al, caused a distraction by starting to clean up some of the debris. The agents started yelling at him about this being a crime scene. Ori and Leslie followed Gus quickly, and the voices started to fade as they passed through the service exit.

"You know, boss, I've seen a lot of people coming in and out of this place for the past fifty years, and something just didn't seem right about those people." Gus said as he leads them through the service entrance hall of the building.

"The FBI agents?" asked Leslie, wondering what else he may have seen.

Gus gave her a confused look.

Ori said, "Gus, you're the man. We appreciate you."

Ori hurried Leslie out of the service hall. She noticed that they are in the very back of the parking deck, far away from the scene of the explosion. Leslie stopped, "Wait . . . wasn't your car blown up? My car is surrounded by agents. How are we going to get out of here?"

"No, that was Hetty's car that blew up. We had an arrangement. I have a separate car on its way for her," Ori said as he continued quickly to the back of the parking lot and pulled keys out of his pocket. Ori extended the keys, and Leslie noticed the yellow taillights on a pickup truck flash as she heard the doors unlock. The two quickly hopped in the vehicle and drove out of the back service exit of the complex.

As the two drove off, Leslie realized that she had never seen Ori drive before. She'd known him for several years and never paid attention to the type of car he drove or that he had a secret escape elevator. She started to wonder what else she didn't know about him.

Ori's phone vibrated as soon as they were in the car and out of the parking deck. He noticed that he had a new text message from the unknown number. He handed his phone to Leslie and asked her to read it.

It said, "I'm assuming you got out of there with your lawyer friend. Don't go home. Call your friend again."

She handed the phone back to him, and Ori quickly pressed one button. The phone started dialing a number, and Ori pressed it to his ear. "Hey," Ori said in a low, stern voice. "Are you good?"

Leslie couldn't make out the phone conversation, and then Ori said, "Hang on, I'm driving. Let me put you on speaker."

Leslie heard a voice that she recognized as Tony's. "Are you guys okay? What the hell happened?"

"Tony! I'd ask the same of you. You've had all of us worried!" exclaimed Leslie.

"Hiiiiii, Leslie," Tony said, being silly at the oddest time, in true Tony fashion.

"We are both okay," Ori answered Tony. "I'm still trying to sort out what happened. What's your status? We need to meet in person. It's not safe at my home, and I'm assuming it's not safe at Leslie's either."

"Yeah, that's a safe bet. I figured that they would have your homes on lockdown. There's a lot to catch you up on, so just come directly to the airport."

"Hartsfield-Jackson?" Leslie asked, puzzled.

Tony replied, "No, the DeKalb-Peachtree Airport. And hurry."

Chapter 16

"Ori, what else is going on? This is freaking me out." Leslie pleaded, "Why the airport? Where are we going? And what was Tony talking about when he said there's a lot to catch you up on?"

"Do you remember a few years ago how Roger and I continued to butt heads on whether to take the company public?" Ori asked.

"Yeah, I clearly remember that," Leslie said, recalling the tension around the topic throughout the company. "Everyone remembers that period. What about it?"

"When we were entertaining the idea of becoming a publicly traded company, I set up regular meetings with Warren and Roger to keep a close eye on our accounting and financials. We wanted to make sure that there were no surprises that could derail the public offering or valuation of the stock if we chose to go that route." Ori continued, "We kept the meetings a secret because we didn't want anyone to change their behavior. About three years ago, Warren started to notice some bizarre behaviors. There were several random payments out of the discretionary expense account to outside accounts. The payments weren't large, relatively speaking. They were mostly between ten thousand and twenty thousand dollars."

"Well, those aren't substantial payments. What made that significant?" Leslie asked.

"The payments were coming from Roger's expense account," Ori said.

"Roger, of course, denied any knowledge of the payments. He claimed to have no clue what they could be or to whom the outside accounts belonged. And I believed him. Roger is a good guy, and he's good with money. If Roger were going to do something illegal or suspicious, he's too smart to do it from his own expense account."

"I don't understand the problem then," Leslie said.

"It's what happened next that became the issue. We needed to figure out what was being purchased, who was making the purchases, and who was the recipient of those funds. Roger agreed not to question any of his people on it until we did a little investigating. We wanted to see if we could catch someone in the act. Maybe a month or two later, Warren noticed that there was a single wire transfer from one of my expense accounts for fifteen thousand dollars that had no documentation. I had Tony look into it, with discretion of course, and two prime suspects came up. The digital footprint pointed to Warren. But Warren told me about the odd payments, so that didn't make any sense to me. Tony pulled some security footage from Warren's office and saw Monica in there after hours one day."

Monica had a very unassuming look, with her wide-rimmed glasses and auburn hair tied usually back tight in a ponytail. She was always well dressed, in a subtle, classy way. Leslie often admired her outfits.

"Monica from the Finance Department?" Leslie asked with genuine surprise. "She's so sweet and cute."

"That's the one," Ori confirmed.

"But wasn't she hired to help with the public offering?" Leslie asked. "Why would she try to sabotage it? She would have made a ridiculous bonus if that deal had gone through."

"That's a good question, and I wasn't quite sure either. So, Tony did more digging, and her background was spotty at best," Ori said.

At a red light, Ori took out his old flip phone and started scrolling through the messages. He pulled up a photo of a man and showed the screen to Leslie. "Does that man look familiar?" In the pictures, Monica appeared to be sitting down and having coffee with a tall man with short hair.

"I can't get a good look at his face," Leslie said.

"You don't really need a good look at his face," Ori said. "Take a look at his wrist."

"What do you mean?" As soon as Leslie asked that question, she noticed the titanium wristband.

"Is that the guy from the meeting with the Wesley Corporation? How long ago was this photo taken?" Leslie asked.

"Almost two years ago. Well before this acquisition was ever proposed," Ori said. "He introduced himself as Silas."

"I don't understand," Leslie said, baffled.

"Well, I didn't either. Since Roger hired Monica, I started to ask him more about her, trying to get to know her a little. Roger became very defensive of her, and he thought that it was inappropriate that I accuse her of anything without hard evidence. He said how highly recommended she had come from a close friend of his whom he respects tremendously." Ori sighed. "I pretended that we were fine, and didn't bring it up with Roger again."

"Do you think he said something to her?" Leslie asked.

"Maybe, but I can't be sure." Ori glanced over at her quickly and then set his eyes back on the road.

"So why do you think that's relevant now? Because of seeing Silas in the Wesley meeting?" Leslie asked.

"I don't understand everything, but Monica is involved. The pieces of this puzzle are starting to come together, and Tony has more information that should add some clarity," Ori said.

"How am I involved in all of this?" Leslie said.

"Since then, in addition to his day job of investigating potential business partnerships, I've provided Tony with a budget to look into Monica and try to understand what the end game is. He started identifying other failed attempts to hurt the company or me."

"Do I even want to know?" Leslie asked.

"Do you?" Ori answered.

"Ugh, you know I have to know," Leslie said.

"Do you remember when I asked you to set up a legal team to offer counsel to the employees in our Legacy program?"

Leslie remembered. "I think that it was so good to offer them legal counsel to make sure that they were fully aware of their rights." Leslie was a huge fan of this program. During her time working at the law firm, she did a lot of volunteer work to help reduce the recidivism rate. Leslie loved how this program was doing that by giving people who were formally incarcerated good jobs and opportunities to develop and grow while providing a safe environment for their families. The program infrastructure was one of the many reasons she loved working for the Singularity Group.

"Those employees really wanted to stay on the right path. Some were more at risk than others," Ori said.

"That's right," Leslie said, thinking back to that period. "There were a few in particular who seemed to meet with the legal team for advice more regularly."

"There was a specific reason for that, and they allowed their lawyers to fill me in. Several guys were constantly getting harassed by local authorities. It was only the ones with connections to a specific criminal organization that had networks in Chicago, LA, and New York. One day, someone approached them, saying that they could get the cops off their backs."

"In exchange for what?" Leslie asked.

"They all worked in our distribution facilities and were asked for their employee entry badges," Ori said. "For doing it, they would each also receive a substantial amount of money."

"Did anyone give access to their badge?" Leslie asked.

"Only under our guidance," Ori said. "Jordan set up a duplicate system with fake data that looked completely real. We needed the perpetrators to feel like they were successful so that we could continue to track them."

"Holy shit, this is intense," said Leslie.

"Whoever used those badges to access our facilities knew what they were doing. They avoided all our cameras so we couldn't get images of their faces. However, since we knew which badges were compromised, we were able to find out who had accessed our HR database. They were pulling employee records, W-2 data, and bank account details." Ori paused, and then explained, "The distribution centers are some of the few facilities that still store employee information on mainframes located on-premise and not in the cloud. We believe that someone accessed the desktops and pulled data on anyone who went to prison on minor drug charges. They also reviewed shipping routes and logistics details.

"Since all the information they received was fake, they did not get any legitimate information. But it was very peculiar that the search history was specifically for employees who had criminal records, particularly those who were found guilty on a narrow set of federal crimes," Ori said.

"After that, the trail got cold. Fast forward, and we asked Tony to investigate the Wesley deal. When he went radio silent, I got worried but didn't quite connect the dots. Then I saw Silas in the Wesley meeting. And then if that wasn't enough of a red flag, I got this odd message warning me that something was wrong, that I needed to get out and bring you with me. I'm not entirely sure how you are involved, but my gut told me to trust the warning. So, I don't know exactly where this is going to lead, but I know that something nefarious is going on." As they arrived at the airstrip, Ori said, "It's up to you if you want to get on that plane with me. If you do, I can assure you that you will be safe, at least for a little while longer, and we will both hopefully get more answers. If not, I can leave you here, and you can decide whether you want to tell the authorities everything that I just told you."

Leslie began to feel a little nauseous as the gravity of the situation began setting in. There had been multiple attempts to damage the company, a bomb went off in the parking lot that was clearly intended for Ori, the FBI seemed suspicious of Ori and had no suspects, yet they were trying to put him into protective custody. Under other circumstances, Leslie would have returned to the building, told the FBI what Ori just told her, and trusted that they would find the truth. But here she was, with her stomach trying to flip upside down, and her intuition screaming something completely different. "You've never lied to me before, and you've always had my best interests in mind. Why would I think that you would change now?" Leslie said, and she opened the car door and headed toward the plane.

As they approached the Learjet, Tony stepped out to meet them. Holding out his hand, Ori turned to her and explained, "Tony needs to reconfigure our phones so that we can't be followed."

Leslie looked at Tony, and he said, "Don't worry, I'm just throwing them off our trail. Hurry, we need to get going." Leslie slowly handed Tony her smartphone and boarded the jet.

Ori was clearly pleased to see Jordan was somehow already there as well. As he gave her a hug, she said, "Your bag is in the overhead compartment."

Tony told them to grab a seat quickly as they needed to leave at once. As Ori and Leslie fastened their seatbelts, Tony went up to the pilots and instructed them to take off.

Ori looked at Jordan. "Did you remember to grab my —
"

"Yes, your laptop is in the bag," she said without taking her eyes off her laptop.

"And what about my —" Ori started.

Jordan then threw him a clear plastic bag with something colorful inside.

"Ah, you're the best," Ori said with a smile as he unrolled the bag and started pulling out gummy bears.

He noticed Leslie looking at him oddly and said with a grin, "Would you like one?"

Tony had rejoined them, and Leslie noticed he looked a little worse for wear.

"Tony," Ori started, staring at his face.

"Give me a minute," Tony said as he looked out of the window anxiously. "Wait until we're up in the air."

Ori nodded and remained quiet.

"Okay," Tony continued a couple of minutes later. "We are clear now. What's up?"

Ori raised his eyebrows at Tony. "Rough week?" He cracked a smile.

"Something like that," Tony said as he let out a laugh and rubbed his hands over his hair.

Chapter 17

Agents Blackwood, Chivington, and Cramer were waiting near the conference room just down the hall from Ori's office. Mikiko walked up. "I have the list of everyone who entered the building over the past couple of weeks as well as video footage."

Mikiko and Evelyn grabbed a seat at the end of the long farm table and began quickly reviewing the names on the list.

In her periphery, Evelyn noticed Agent Chivington look over to Agent Cramer and asked, "Do you know what Clayborn was talking about with that breach comment?"

"It sounded like some self-righteous nonsense to me," Cramer said. "What did he say, that he's repairing the breach? What breach?"

"He was referring to Isaiah fifty-eight verse twelve from the King James Version of the Bible," Evelyn said without looking up. "And they that shall be of thee shall build the old waste places: thou shalt raise up the foundations of many generations; and thou shalt be called, The repairer of the breach, The restorer of paths to dwell in." Evelyn then looked to Mikiko. "Have you looked at the video footage yet?"

"Yes, we looked at footage of the parking deck. There was a black sports utility vehicle that arrived on the premises shortly before the explosion and left immediately after the bomb was detonated," Mikiko said.

"That's great," Cramer said.

"Not quite," Mikiko continued. "We were not able to get the license plate number, so we don't have any details to track the vehicle, and the cameras didn't get a good look at the driver."

"It's been almost an hour," Chivington said. "Do you want to go and check on him?"

"Sure," Cramer said and headed toward Ori's office. No more than a few minutes later, they heard him shout, "Dammit!"

They rushed after him into the office to realize that no one was there. They quickly dispersed, searching every conference room and bathroom.

"Dammit, he's not here," Chivington said. "Do you think he left the building?"

"We've got guys all over the place, and no one has reported seeing him leave," said Mikiko.

"Where's the attorney and Clayborn's assistant?" asked Evelyn.

"No sign of them either," Mikiko said.

"We've missed something. We need to find where Clayborn went, and now," Cramer said. "They did not just vanish into thin air. I need to brief the section chief."

They went downstairs and found the lead GBI agent.

"Were there any vehicles that left the premises within the past hour?" Evelyn asked.

"I just checked, and it looks like there was only a pickup truck that exited out of the back service exit of the parking deck," he said.

"I bet that was him," Evelyn said.

"What do you mean?" asked Chivington.

"Clayborn was always a modest guy. If that luxury car wasn't his," she gestured to the debris, "then I bet that pickup truck was. We need to get back to the command center. They already have a huge head start."

Back at the command center, the team was surprised to see Section Chief Appleton waiting for them. Mikiko and Evelyn went straight to work searching through footage, using the latest facial recognition technology, for a clue as to where Ori may have gone.

"What are you doing here, sir?" Chivington asked.

"I want to be close to this; this is a big case. Based on what I'm hearing, it's already getting out of control," Appleton said.

"No hits on Clayborn or the attorney on any of the cameras," Mikiko announced.

"I didn't think we'd be that lucky," Evelyn replied.

"However, a private plane did just depart from Dekalb Airport. It's registered under a subsidiary company owned by Clayborn," Mikiko said.

"Where's it heading?" Cramer asked.

"The flight plan says that it's going to the Virgin Islands," Mikiko said.

"Sir," Cramer chimed in, "that flight plan aligns with data we are picking up from their cell phones."

"Ha," Appleton laughed. "These people always think that they are so smart. What idiots."

"Why would he be going to the Virgin Islands?" Evelyn asked. "Something doesn't make sense."

"We pulled his records. One of his subsidiary companies owns a massive yacht in the US Virgin Islands. It's probably stocked with enough rations to survive for a year at sea. I bet he plans to go into hiding on a boat," Cramer suggested.

"Let's go get him before that happens," Appleton exclaimed.

As all of the agents started quickly packing up their gear to move, Evelyn stood there looking at information on her computer.

"Section Chief Appleton," Evelyn said.

"Yes, Agent Blackwood," he replied with vague interest.

Evelyn continued, "Something is not right. It doesn't make sense that he would go through all of this trouble to escape to somewhere we could easily follow him."

"Agent Blackwood, green is not a good color on you. Just because *you* weren't the one to find him doesn't mean the lead is wrong," Cramer said.

"It's just a stupid move, and this guy is anything but stupid," Evelyn said.

"See, that's your problem, Agent Blackwood. You give these people too much credit. Stay here if you don't want to come," Appleton said.

The team started to head out while Evelyn and Mikiko watched. "You need to go with them," Evelyn said. "Even though my gut is telling me that Clayborn isn't heading to the Virgin Islands, I think that it's important that one of us stay close to the section chief. I don't trust him or his people."

"What are you going to do?" Mikiko asked.

"Interestingly enough, I'm seeing a separate flight that left just minutes before. It was heading in a different direction. I'll head that way and keep you posted."

Chapter 18

Once the plane climbed to altitude, the pilot gave the signal that they could move around the cabin if they wanted.

Tony stood a couple of inches shorter than Ori at an athletic five feet, ten inches. He had once admitted to Leslie that his thick-framed glasses and slightly baggy clothes were selected to intentionally lead people to underestimate how lethal he could be. He was brilliant with coding and very intelligent. When he was in the service, Tony did a lot of special assignments, typically highly restricted solo missions. He had to learn ways to remain disarming and conceal his extensive defense training. Everything about his appearance was by design so that he could easily blend in and infiltrate however needed.

Tony and Ori had known each other for quite a while. Leslie wasn't sure exactly how they forged a friendship, but she did know that they had a shared passion for boxing, Brazilian jiu-jitsu, and Krav Maga.

Leslie noticed Ori assessing Tony. Finally he said, "So did you run into Dean or what?"

Tony started laughing so hard his body began to shake. He grabbed his ribs, clearly still in pain.

Ori looked over at Leslie and explained, "Overzealous guy from the boxing gym." He then looked to Tony, nodded toward his ribs and asked, "Are they broken?"

"Just bruised," Tony said. "My ribs and my ego. I'm still not sure what happened. Two men, highly skilled, jumped me at the MARTA station," Tony said, rubbing the back of his head.

"Did you get a good look at them?" Ori asked.

"No, they were wearing masks," Tony said, "but they had to have been military trained, Special Forces potentially."

"Why would they attack you?" Leslie asked.

"That's a great question and something that we need to figure out," Tony replied.

Everyone was quiet for a few minutes.

Leslie broke the silence "Where are we going? And how do we know we'll be safe there?"

Jordan took out her laptop and turned it on. "Right now, we have the pilots on a course for Mexico, and from there, I've made arrangements to get us someplace safe."

"Do we know exactly what kind of trouble we are in and why?" Leslie asked.

Ori looked at Tony, "What were you able to find out?"

"Where do I begin?" Tony looked at Leslie. "Do we all know about the Monica situation?"

She nodded.

Tony continued, "That was the first of several attempts to set the company up."

"You're referring to Project Legacy?" Leslie assumed.

"Good, I see Ori briefed you," Tony replied.

"Ori told me about that. Those employees worked in the distribution centers, right?" Leslie said.

"That's correct, in our Los Angeles, New York, and Chicago distribution centers," Tony said. "What's interesting is that all of them went down on relatively petty drug possession charges."

Leslie was not sure why that was so interesting. About fifty percent of the workers in the program had been arrested for the first time with a small amount of pot on them. To make a case for the prosecutors, the arresting officer would tell some story about them being a drug dealer for the largest gang in the area at the time. Politicians loved bragging about all the arrests that they were making to take down dangerous drug dealers, when in many cases these were high school kids buying pot for a party.

"The interesting thing," Tony said, as if reading her thoughts, "is that the bosses of the three criminal organizations that these employees were allegedly affiliated with have all gone missing."

"How long ago?" Ori asked.

"I'm not quite sure," Tony said. "But looks to be within the past year." He continued, "You know these guys typically keep a low profile, but my sources told me that about a year ago, violence spiked in their territories. There were some brutal murders of key people in their organizations. Then the streets went quiet, and it was business as usual."

"Hmmm . . ." Ori said, "How brutal?"

"Think severed heads on spikes."

Leslie gasped and covered her mouth in disgust.

"And there was not one word about this in the news?" Jordan asked.

"People were pretty spooked," Tony said. "No one on the streets was talking. And anyone in the media who decided to look into the killings was sent eyes, a tongue, and a note saying 'Siempre te estoy mirando,' or 'I'm always watching you'."

"Is that who's after us?" Leslie asked, feeling panicked. "Oh my God," she whispered under her breath.

"I don't think so," Ori said. "If the person after us is capable of doing the things that Tony is saying, then we would be dead by now."

"I think someone wants to make it seem like that's who is after us," Tony agreed.

"So, who are they pointing the finger to? Who is that violent?" Leslie asked, feeling incapable of taking all this in.

"La Tiniebla Cartel, I would guess," Jordan said without looking up from her computer. "They are the only ones bold, brutal, and ruthless enough to do something like that in the US." Jordan looked up. "We also found out that fake nonprofit organizations were founded under Ori's name and used as a front to fund various terrorist organizations."

"What? Did you alert the authorities? How did I not know this?" Leslie asked.

"We thought it was best to keep you out of this since the organizations were not affiliated with the Singularity Group. We did let our contact inside one of the agencies know, and they were tracking it," Jordan said.

"You have a contact inside a government agency?" Leslie thought at some point this conversation would get less surprising.

"There is a bigger game at play," Ori said, ignoring Leslie's last question.

"I obviously started with Monica to try to understand more about who could be behind this," Tony said. "On the surface, all of her information checks out. But when I tried to pull historical information on her, it is as if she never existed seven years ago."

"More to come on that." Tony paused, rubbing the side of his ribs in pain as he grimaced, then continued, "So then,

Jordan and I started monitoring the dark web and noticed a lot of internet activity that appeared to be set up and run by Ori. Things like inquiring about illegal firearms, government documents, money laundering. This account didn't do anything illegal yet, but it was as if someone was trying to leave breadcrumbs that would lead back to Ori slowly."

"No way that would hold up in court," Leslie exclaimed.

"It all depends on the political agenda of the time," Ori said, "and whose agenda I'm disrupting. And it depends on how the false evidence stacks up against the truth. There are plenty of cases where everyone knew the defendant was being framed, where key witnesses were facing twenty years of prison time, or critical evidence had huge gaps. You wonder how some of those defendants were found guilty, but they were."

"They would have a convincing case against Ori," added Tony. He looked over at Leslie. "Let's be real. If the things that are happening to Ori are what we think they are, and Ori is arrested and tried in a courtroom, this battle will be fought in the media and public opinion. If Ori is painted as a criminal mastermind, with falsified data to back that claim, he will lose all the positive press and attention that he's gained over the years. All of this will translate in the court to a guilty verdict."

"How do you know all of this, Tony?" Leslie gazed at Tony questioningly.

Tony looked down, "This is what I was trained to perfect."

"It wouldn't matter if I'm found guilty or not guilty; the damage to the Singularity Group's reputation would have been done," Ori said.

"So, you believe that the FBI is trying to frame Ori for drugs and terrorism?" Leslie's voice raised an octave.

"I don't know if it's the FBI or not. I don't think that they are trying to link him to a terrorist cell. But this is the approach I would take if I were setting someone up for a massive fall. A very public fall. It's one of the few ways you can destroy someone who is credible and has resources. You claim that all of their financials are tied to illegal activities, so they shouldn't be able to access them."

"There goes your great legal team," Jordan chimed in.

Tony continued, "Then, they make anyone credible with a good reputation fear associating themselves with you."

"Because no one wants to be affiliated with a drug-dealing, arms-buying terrorist," Jordan added.

"If they decided to blow up a car that they thought I was driving," Ori said, "I'm not sure they plan on allowing this to play out in the courts."

Tony shook his head and then continued. "After we discovered the bread crumbs, we kept following them until the trail went cold. I've been monitoring the clues ever since, but we haven't seen any movement in at least six months. Then, Ori asked me to look into this Wesley

Corporation deal. I thought it was a routine background check, but I was completely wrong. If I were a betting man, I would bet everything I own that the Wesley deal is the start of something bigger."

"It's you that they are after, and your credibility," Leslie said, getting a handle on things for the first time. "First, the odd wire transfers from the company by one of your senior leaders and top confidants. Then, those Legacy Program members get approached for their badges. Then, the leaders of their gangs go missing in an apparent drug turf war. Dark web activity to point toward terrorist activities. Lastly, there's an attempt on your life." Leslie came to a sickening realization. "It seems like someone does want you dead, based on the bombing, but it's more than that. They want to ruin your legacy."

Jordan stopped typing, and all three of them are looking at Leslie with an odd look on their faces, something a little like satisfaction or pride. Leslie decided to continue, "We need to figure out who is behind this and why."

Ori smiles, "Yes, *we* do, and we need to keep *you* safe."

Chapter 19

"Do you think it's really happening?" Jordan asked.

"I wanted to be absolutely sure, and as I started doing more digging, I saw familiar faces in unfamiliar places," Tony said. "I was getting close to something, and I realized that I needed to set things in motion to get off the grid and to get you guys off the grid too."

"I had my suspicions. Something about this deal seemed off. Just too perfect, you know?" Ori said.

"I started poking around the town where the Wesley Corporation has its headquarters and looking into the Wesley brothers. I found out that Milton was quite the partier in his youth. He had no problem throwing his money and power around the small town. As a result, his son grew to be a piece of work, your typical rich kid. Just like his father, he loved to party, and he loved women. He developed a bad reputation very young. Then he met a mysterious woman who turned out to be connected to a major cartel and was looking to escape somewhere in Middle America. The cartel came looking for her, and

Milton Jr. agreed to exchange some favors if they let her go. Milton Jr. ran the transportation business unit."

Tony paused before explaining further, "As you know, they manage a massive fleet of semitrucks and an expansive distribution network. With Milton Jr. overseeing the trucking business, he was a target. The next thing you know, one of the largest cartels is using the Wesley Corporation's trucking business to transport everything from drugs, humans, and weapons across the United States. The DEA has been watching this play out for two to three years. Then something goes down, and one of their trucks gets pulled over unplanned. One of those real coincidental situations, but nevertheless, it was a huge bust for some small-town cops."

"Wait, what? How did we not know about this?" Leslie asked. "This should have definitely come up as our team was researching the company."

"It would have come up if it were ever officially reported. I had to get a few local police officers drunk for them to divulge this information. But, as soon as the bust happened, the DEA and FBI swarmed in and took over the case. I checked with some old resources at the Bureau, and even they didn't know about this."

"It's not uncommon for some law enforcement agencies to use busts like that to expand their network of informants and other assets," Jordan said, still typing away on her computer.

"Oh, just wait for the kicker. You would never guess who the mysterious woman was," Tony said, with a sharp look in his eyes.

The group was quiet, waiting in suspense.

"We knew her as Monica. She was going by the name Nicole up there," Tony said.

"That's not her name either," Ori said, unsurprised by Tony's news. "Her name is Jackeline Gutierrez de la Cruz, and I knew her father."

Leslie stared at Ori with surprise and confusion painted on her face. He continued, "I knew him when I was a just a kid; we studied together. Then years later, we were reunited through a chance encounter during which I also met his very young daughter, Jackeline. When I saw Monica, she immediately reminded me of Angel, as well as Jackeline. However, I didn't think it could possibly be the same person. You see, Jackeline had ocular albinism. The little girl I knew was almost completely blind."

"Who's Angel?" Leslie asked.

"Angel Carlos Gutierrez de La Cruz," Ori said.

"There is no evidence to support this, but he is suspected of heading La Tiniebla Cartel," Jordan explained.

Ori looked at Tony, "An FBI agent asked me about my connection with La Tiniebla."

"That's either a giant leap or very suspicious," Tony said.

"Things aren't what they seem," Ori said. "No one who would say anything knows I have a connection with Carlos."

Leslie asked, "Where is Jackeline now? We probably need to speak with her."

"She wasn't at work this week," Jordan answered.

"I was just about to tell you. We can't speak with her," Tony said as his face turned a bit grim. "The police were checking everyone's alibis around the time of the explosion, starting with the people who didn't come into the office. The police apparently found a lot of blood at Jackeline's apartment."

"Oh, my goodness," whispered Leslie.

"Is she dead?" Jordan asked.

"According to my connection at the police department." Tony's voice dropped. "Her apartment apparently looked like a slaughterhouse."

"Do you think her dad did it?" Jordan asked.

"No," Ori said sternly. Then his voice softened to a normal tone. "I met Carlos before he was the myth that you think of today. The young man that I knew was quite different. I knew him when we were both younger before we both fully embraced our paths. I know the type of person Carlos is. He's the type of man that doesn't feel the need to lie to anyone about anything. And he would never hurt his daughter."

Ori looked at Leslie. "When we had the accounting errors and found the footage of Monica in Roger's office, I decided to say something myself. I might not have, except I still wondered if she was actually Jackeline after all."

"Wow, how did that go?" asked Leslie

"I told her what we had seen. Told her we valued her as an employee, and if she were in some kind of trouble that I could help with, to please tell me."

"She apologized for what she was doing. She said that a friend was in trouble with dangerous people and needed her to do him a favor. If she hadn't done it, then they would kill him. She seemed terrified. She promised never to do anything compromising again, and she begged me to give her another chance."

"Then?" Leslie asked.

"I decided to call Carlos. I sent him a picture, and he confirmed that it was his daughter. I asked him if she was in danger, and he said he had an eye on her. In fact, he asked me if I could let her continue working here. I trust him, so I allowed it, and Jackeline stopped making the transactions."

"Did Monica know her dad knew where she was?" Jordan asked.

"No," Ori said. "I'm positive."

Ori rubbed his chin. "So we are dealing with someone who knew who Monica was and chose to use her to set me up."

"Do you think they know who Carlos is?" Jordan asked.

"If someone used his daughter to get to me, then I would assume that they know who Carlos is. But they definitely don't know who Carlos *really* is. If they did, they would make sure that they are far out of his reach." Ori said, starting to pace down the airplane aisle.

Tony nodded. "For someone to risk pissing off Carlos to frame you, that means they are either desperate or dumb."

Ori looked out a window, slightly tilting his head. "Or they think that they are incredibly smart," Ori said.

Ori started laughing out of nowhere. Leslie looked at him, puzzled.

"They never knew," Ori said, mystified. "They never knew that I had a connection to Monica." He caught himself. "Jackeline." Ori paused. "I need to make a call. Tony, you keep playing out the scenario with Jordan and Leslie," Ori said as he moved to the far back of the cabin.

"So, we believe that getting Ori to acquire the Wesley Corporation is the final play in the plan. With the bread crumbs that Monica left behind, this would have completed a perfect story of how Ori is involved in the drug business." Tony's voice filled with gravity. "I can read the headline now: 'Ori Clayborn, Billionaire Founder of the Singularity Group, Indicted'."

Leslie jumped in, "And they would probably try to pin the death of Monica or Nicole or Jackeline, whatever her name is, on him too."

"Yep. We've been able to identify the what." Tony sighed. "We're going to need help to identify the who."

"The big ending, huh," Jordan said, her demeanor suddenly turning sad. Jordan exhaled a deep, long sigh. "I guess all good things must come to an end."

"We've all known that this day would come. Now we stick to the plan," Ori said, walking back in. "It's time to go see the professor."

"The professor?" Leslie asked.

"He is one of my mentors. He helped me flesh out the early ideas of our business model," Ori said. "For lack of a better word, he is the most knowledgeable historian on Earth."

"Does he specialize in any particular field?" Leslie asked.

"All fields," Ori and Jordan said simultaneously.

"Where is the professor?" Leslie asked.

"Northwest," Ori said simply.

"Well, let's do it, team," Tony said, heading toward the cockpit.

Chapter 20

"We just got a message from the local authorities at the airport in the US Virgin Islands. They have Clayborn's airplane surrounded and are awaiting instruction from us before they engage," Agent Chivington said.

"Good. And you've confirmed that no one has left the plane?" Section Chief Appleton asked.

"Affirmative, sir," Chivington responded.

"We've got him now," Appleton smiled.

As the federal task force's plane landed, the agents swiftly deboarded the plane and moved toward the private jet, with their firearms drawn. The confused faces of the jet's pilots were visible as the agents surrounded the plane. The pilots did as they were told and opened the boarding door.

Agent Chivington barked orders at the pilots, "Shut the engine down and put your hands where I can see them." The other agents got into position near the open door of the plane. Once the other agents were in place, Chivington continued yelling, "All passengers, get off of the plane now."

The agents waited for what seemed like an eternity. They stared at the opening of the Learjet, waiting anxiously for some movement. There was nothing.

"You do not want us to come on there and force you out," Chivington yelled again.

Mikiko looked at the pilots and noticed that they were looking at each other and shrugging their shoulders. After another minute of no movement, Mikiko followed her gut and asked, "Special Agent Chivington, permission to board the plane?"

"Negative, you sit back." Chivington pointed to two other agents and used his index and middle finger to signal them to board the aircraft. Once the agents vanished inside the cabin, Mikiko and the others watched intently for some sign of trouble. Seconds later, the agents on the ground received a message in their earpiece, "All clear. Only the two pilots are on board."

The two agents escorted the two pilots off with their hands still raised in the air.

Chivington went to speak with the pilots. Mikiko then trailed Appleton onto the plane to have a look around. There were two cell phones in two of the passenger seats. One phone had an unread text message.

Mikiko quickly referenced the contact list from the explosion investigation and then dialed Ori's number.

"This one is Clayborn's," she said and pointed to the phone with the unread message.

"The other must belong to the attorney," Appleton said.

Mikiko watched as he slipped on a single white rubber glove and picked up the phones. "Agent Cramer!" he called.

"Yes, sir?" Cramer shuffled over from the cockpit.

"Get both phones back to the lab. I want to know everything they were up to."

Mikiko noticed that after Agent Cramer placed the phones in separate bags, he gave an analyst Leslie's phone but slipped Ori's phone in his jacket pocket. She thought it was odd, and made a mental note to tell Evelyn once they could have a secure conversation.

The section chief looked at Mikiko. "Agent Shikibu, let's go find out what the pilots have to say." They walked back off the plane and found Agent Chivington wrapping up a conversation with the pilots.

Chivington turned to Mikiko and Appleton. "They were told to come here to pick up some people."

"Did they say who?" Appleton asked.

"They were told that they'd be picking up some FBI agents as part of something highly confidential."

Appleton turned red with frustration. "What the hell kind of game is this?" he shouted.

As he stormed away to call the deputy director and provide an update, Mikiko stepped away from the group as well to call Evelyn. "You nailed it. This was a distraction. There were a couple of cell phones found that we believe belong to Clayborn and Ochoa. They are taking them back to the lab for analysis. Anything on your end?"

"Nothing yet, and I'm afraid I've missed my window," replied Evelyn. "I believe that Ori was here, but there's no trace of his next steps. If he got a boat, it would be next to impossible to find them. The good news is that he is still in North America, at least for the moment. I'll take the next flight back to Atlanta, and we can regroup there. We should be able to leverage our friends at the NSA to see what information they can provide. I don't think he's trying to run."

Chapter 21

"El Caído." One of Carlos's men approached him as he slipped his cell phone back into his jacket pocket. "Victor just called. El Ruso should be here any minute."

"Must be important if they can't wait until the next meeting," Carlos mused.

Carlos looked over at the man. "Have El Ruso meet me in my office when he gets here, por favor."

El Ruso was a surprisingly small man for a name like El Ruso. He was balding and always had a pair of reading glasses hanging around his neck. Most who came across him would think that he was an accountant. Carlos liked Victor's second in command; he was brilliant. El Ruso spent a lot of his formative years studying human thought and behavior, focusing on how to influence and exercise control over other human beings. Because of his physical stature, he needed to outthink his rivals to get to the position that he is in now.

El Ruso walked into the office a bit later. Carlos waved his hand to the guard, motioning for him to leave the two alone.

As soon as the door closed, Carlos said, "Kazimir, my friend, it is great to see you. Please have a seat with me."

Kazimir sat down and started by inquiring, "Estamos seguros?"

"Oh, yes, this room is completely secure. Would you like a drink?" Carlos said.

"Yes, please. It has been an intense few months," Kazimir replied.

"I have a wonderful bottle of wine that I've been waiting to open. But I'm sensing this is more of a whiskey or vodka conversation," Carlos said with a slight smile.

"Give me a glass of that tequila you try to keep hidden," Kazimir smiled knowingly.

Carlos poured them each a glass and returned to sit across from Kazimir. "Salud!" they both said as they clinked their glasses.

"So, what brings you all the way over here in such a hurry?" Carlos asked.

"I think that we may have a problem. I think that someone is trying to come at the corporation," Kazimir said.

"What do you mean, Kazimir?" Carlos raised his eyebrows, thinking Kazimir was most likely overreacting, though that wasn't typical for him. Staying nonchalant, he continued, "Who would try such a thing?"

"I'm serious," Kazimir said. "I think there's a new player. Someone with expansive connections. We think he was behind the hits on your major distribution leaders."

Carlos felt his own posture stiffening. "Do you have a name for this new player? I would very much like to have a chat with them."

Kazimir continued, "The name I've been given is Ori Clayborn. I had not heard of him before, but he appears to be an extremely wealthy man with broad legitimate businesses that give him a great deal of cover for his other endeavors."

"I actually know that name very well," Carlos said. "He is all over the business journals. But why would someone in his position try to come after the corporation and me?" Carlos asked.

"That's the thing; I don't have the slightest idea," Kazimir said.

"How did you get his name?" Carlos asked with a stone-cold expression.

"I'm telling you this because I consider you a friend. We have done a lot of remarkable things together, and I think that there is still a lot left in this relationship," Kazimir said.

"Yes, of course." Carlos tried to soften his expression.

"Once we found out that the three key players of your US operations were hit, we did some digging on our own.

We knew that from the outside looking in, we might be the most logical people to do something like that. But it wasn't us, and we needed to know who else would have the balls to come after you so brutally. We identified a couple of small-time guys who managed nightclubs and a few other front businesses for us. It took a little convincing, but we discovered that they were offered an opportunity to make a name for themselves and run the US operations. At first, they, of course, claimed to not know any names. But we applied our pressure, and the man who approached them with this excellent opportunity mentioned Ori." Kazimir took a sip of his tequila and continued, "Now, clearly, since these guys were loosely affiliated with us, we took care of them. Part of the reason I am here is to let you know that we did not order this. I'm also here to talk through how you want to handle this new player and to find out what support we can offer."

Carlos waited in silence, processing the information. "I take it that you have since asked around about Ori Clayborn?"

"That is correct," Kazimir said.

"Have you heard or found anything else that would make you believe that he would be behind this?" Carlos asked.

"Not beyond this," Kazimir said. "I get the sense that you might know more about this man than I do. Do you think he has the capacity to do something like this?"

Carlos smiled. "Ori Clayborn has the capacity to do anything that he wants. But would he do this? Absolutely not."

"How are you so sure, Carlos?" Kazimir asked.

"Our history is intertwined, one could say. There are few people who I would consider to be friends. In fact, I can count on one hand how many people I would consider to be friends. And hell," Carlos laughed "I may not even need all my fingers. Ori is one of those friends who is to never be touched."

"If he is implicated in disrupting the corporation's business, will that be enough to convince the other board members to leave him alone?"

"As chairman of the board, I have faith that I can persuade them," Carlos said.

"Exercising the chairman of the board position is risky in this situation. Members could think that it's you who is trying to break up the corporation," Kazimir said.

"I will have to help them see the larger picture. This corporation has been making us all very wealthy, and we don't have to look over our shoulders anymore," Carlos said. "Peace generates more profits than carnage and war. Why would I put our peace of mind in jeopardy?"

"Cheers to that," said Kazimir as he raised his glass and drained the rest of his tequila.

"Would you like another?" Carlos asked.

"Why not, just a small one," Kazimir replied. As he got his refill, he asked, "So if not Ori, then who?"

Carlos considered this carefully, and then said, "This is something different, something dark."

Chapter 22

Nicolas was anxiously waiting in the back booth of the dark bar for his guests to arrive. Once they showed up and sat down, he immediately asked, "So did it work? Am I done?"

"Not yet," Appleton said. "We need to see this through to the end."

"Come on, man," he shouted anxiously. "You keep saying that we need to see this through to the end, but the end never comes. You have been telling me that for years now, *Jeremy,*" Nicolas said the section chief's first name with disdain. "What's up with you, man?"

"We'll tell you when we are finished with you. We are close to getting Carlos out of the way," Silas said. "Trust us."

Nicolas laughed and said with disbelief, "Trust you? *Trust you?*" He looked at Appleton. "You have a very short memory, *Jeremy,*" he said, emphasizing the section chief's first name again. "You are in your role because of me. What you have, you owe to me."

"That's enough, Nicolas," said Appleton with spite in his voice, his neck growing red.

"Apparently it's not," snapped Nicolas. "I clearly need to remind you that it was me who saved you from being arrested during the police bust at your favorite underground whorehouse." The section chief tried to shut him up, but Nicolas refused to be quieted. "And it was me who introduced you to Carlos and brokered the deal that got you your big promotion to become section chief."

"That's enough," Silas said again in a low, calm voice, with a slightly bored expression on his face. The section chief was clenching his teeth, trying to keep some form of composure.

"You made a promise that I would be leading La Tiniebla, and I don't think you're keeping your end of the bargain."

"Nicolas, you have to trust me; we're working on it," Appleton said.

"Work faster. Eventually, Carlos is going to find out that you," Nicolas paused, "*we* are behind all of this. What is the plan for me in the meantime?"

"We are in the process of getting you new identification documents, cash, and a business in South Africa that can act as a front and be your source of income. Carlos doesn't have a big presence there, so you should be able to remain safe as long as you keep a low profile," Silas answered.

"Ok, bien, muy bien. I've always wanted to go on a safari." Nicolas grinned, temporarily satisfied. "I will be happy to read about your big bust from there. What's the next play then?"

"For now, you just need to go back to your place and lay low until we reach out," Silas said.

"Of course," Nicolas winked an eye and gave a crooked smile. "But while we're here, let me ask you, what did that Ori guy have to do with any of this? Doesn't seem like a very believable fall guy if you ask me."

"That's none of your concern," Appleton said quickly, trying to calm him down.

Nicolas laughed. "*Jeremy*," he said with the tone of a concerned mother, "you've got to grow a thicker skin. I'm not judging you; in fact, I appreciate you for who you are." Nicolas enjoyed making the section chief uncomfortable. He took a deep and exaggerated sigh. "I truly hope you know what you are doing. Carlos is vicious, but the man has principles. I'd bet anything that Carlos wouldn't appreciate it if he found out that he was not only getting betrayed, but he was also being used as a pawn, especially to set up some random, innocent guy. If," Nicolas paused, "no, when he finds out what you guys are doing..." Nicolas let the possibility hang in the air. Then he looked down and shook his head. "I don't even want to know what he will do to you. I wouldn't be surprised if you end up in Las Cuevas. Carlos loves making examples out of people."

"The Caves?" Silas asked, starting to look less bored. "What are you talking about?"

"Ah, Captain America, Jeremy didn't tell you about the caves." Nicolas said with a sly smile.

"Carlos has a unique way of punishing people who he thinks betrayed him and abandoned his 'vision,'" Nicolas said, making air quotes. "See, Carlos likes to make the punishment fit the crime. A bit biblical if you ask me. If someone gets greedy and steals, Carlos takes their hand and their wealth. He wants them to feel what it is like to have nothing, so that they will appreciate what they have. You know, if they talk too much, then he takes their tongue and blackballs them until he believes they've learned their lesson. Carlos can make someone more of an outcast than you can imagine. One time, a guy went two years without having a conversation with anyone besides his wife and kids. But that's not the worst of it. For someone who really upset Carlos, he short circuits their brain," Nicolas said, and even his game of torturing the section chief couldn't keep the chill from going down his spine at the thought.

"What do you mean, shorts circuits their brain?" Appleton asked.

Small beads of sweat collected on Nicolas's forehead, and his breathing became faster. He continued, "I mean he literally sticks a knife or something in their brain, and the next thing you know, they are wondering around mindless, following his commands like fucking zombies. It's creepy," Nicolas said, staring off.

"Have you seen this yourself?" Silas asked.

"Well he doesn't exactly do it himself. The doctor does. I've seen people go back to his operating room — that's the nickname we gave it — and when they came out, zombies," Nicolas said, feeling dread rising in his chest.

"He performed lobotomies on people?" Appleton asked.

"The ones who get the slice are the ones who try to fool Carlos. You know, like corrupt politicians and police who double-cross him." Nicolas made eye contact with Appleton. "One of your bosses is there. Some big wig from your agency. He promised Carlos something in exchange for a favor. Carlos fulfilled his part of the deal, but your guy changed his mind." Nicolas pushed his index finger against his forehead. "He's now grazing the caverns with the rest of them. Barry something?"

"Wait, are you talking about Section Chief Barry?" Silas said.

"Yeah, that's his name," Nicolas nods. "Section Chief Frank Barry, dirty as they come. So sad and predictable, hmm?" He looked at the current section chief with meaning. "He was on Carlos's payroll for years. Word on the street was that Barry was having a little extramarital affair and ended up getting the woman pregnant. The other woman, Cecilia, I believe, happened to be married to some senior fed official. Tsk, tsk, am I right?"

"Cecelia Gomez? Shit!" Appleton started to see the story.

"Gomez, that was her name." Nicolas said. "Cecilia wanted to leave her husband for Barry, but Barry didn't share the same feelings. Cecilia threatened to tell her husband, which would cost Barry his career, so he asked El Jefe for a favor. Quite the ask, hmm?" Nicolas said, enjoying the incredulous looks on the section chief's and Silas's faces. "Have you heard this story?"

Appleton started, "The Gómezes' died in a car —"

"Car accident," Nicolas cut him off. "They lost control of their car and slammed into a wall. Carlos had some people hack into their vehicle system and take control of the car."

"That's a shame; Gomez had a solid reputation," Silas said.

"Don't feel bad for Gomez. He had his demons too: a thing for young boys. Rumor had it that his wife, Cecilia, knew and was never concerned as long as she lived a life of luxury," Nicolas said with disgust. "They were a sick couple, man."

"So, Carlos played his part, but when Barry gained power, he forgot how he got there," Nicolas said, shaking his head. "When you make an agreement, a covenant, with

La Tiniebla Cartel, it can never be broken. El Caído owns you."

"You sound scared. Why did you agree to work with us?" Silas asked.

"Because I have dreams too. I have a vision. Carlos will never give up power. The only way to end Carlos's reign is by having a large, well-funded government like the US take him out," Nicolas said, a little uncomfortable saying that aloud.

A little slow on the uptake, Appleton asked, "Wait, but back up. Are you saying that Frank Barry is still alive?"

"Last time I was there, he was still alive," Nicolas said.

"How many others are there?" Silas asked.

"I lost count. You'd be surprised how many people are stupid enough to betray Carlos," Nicolas said.

"Uh—" Silas started, but before he could say anything, Nicolas interjected.

"Yeah, I know what you're thinking. But there's a difference; I'm not stupid."

"Where is this place? We should find them," Silas said.

"Good luck with that. These people are wandering in some caverns in mountains you don't know. Also, do you think Carlos will just let you walk in and out of there?"

"We can get a warrant or get a Special Forces team in there," Appleton responded.

"Are you kidding me? Do you know . . ." Nicolas started way too loudly and then lowered his voice again. "What

Carlos does with people who he feels betray him is no secret. People high enough in your government know this, and they keep their mouths shut. Why? Because Carlos keeps the peace. Carlos doesn't care if you know what he does to people. He wants people to know that he will always collect on what people offer in order to do business with him — their souls."

"Why not just kill them?" Silas asked.

"Carlos believes that death is too good for some people. Death is tranquil. It's a release from this physical world. He says that welcoming death allows the energy of a corrupted spirit to leave this realm and spread throughout all existence, corrupting anything that it comes into contact with." Nicolas noticed Silas and Appleton stared at him with a blank face and laughed. "Did you assume Carlos was just another criminal that you could easily force out with the same old tactics? The more um . . ." Nicolas paused, searching for the right word, "devout people in the towns have nicknamed him El Caído for a reason. If you spend time in los pueblos, you'll learn that people think Carlos has been charged with guarding the gates of the underworld."

Appleton scoffs. "That's nonsense. You people will believe anything."

"Trust me, I know. It's pretty bizarre stuff. But hey, I've heard rumors of some crazy things happening. And Carlos really believes in this evil spirit energy stuff, man. So,"

Nicolas took a deep breath, "if you don't want a nut job like that running the most notorious criminal organization on Earth, then follow through on what you promised me. Help me become the new head of the cartel."

Chapter 23

Leslie found herself forgetting about all the potential danger that she may face. She was captivated by the beautiful landscape surrounding her as the boat they were in navigated between the various islands off Canada's Pacific coastline. She looked back inside the boat and saw Tony focusing intently on steering the vessel while Jordan acted as his navigator. Leslie looked over at Ori, who looked relaxed, leaning back with sunglasses on as if he was suntanning without a care in the world.

"I love being out here around nature," Ori said, as if he could hear her thoughts.

"I can see that. It's pleasant out here," Leslie replied with a smile. "So, who is this professor?"

"He was someone I met when I was young. He took me under his wing and tried to help me understand and maximize my potential," Ori said, face tilted up to the sky with his eyes closed.

"When was the last time you saw him?"

"It's been a while, but we find ways to stay connected. The professor likes to stay in the know on everything." Ori looked over at Leslie. "Don't be alarmed if he knows a lot about you. That can startle people sometimes."

As Ori turned to face the sky again, Leslie thought, *What did this professor know about her and who else has Ori brought here?*

Leslie considered asking but was distracted as she realized they were slowly approaching a thick fog cloud that appeared to be floating on the water. Quicker than she would have thought, they were surrounded by the fog on all sides, and the only thing she could see was her companions. Jordan and Tony were navigating through the water as if nothing had changed. Leslie, who was starting to become nervous, turned to Ori, whose gaze was still skyward. "Can they see through this fog? It's really thick."

"Jordan's been here countless times; they'll be all right," Ori replied without looking at Leslie. Perhaps sensing that she was still uneasy, Ori added, "Trust me, nothing bad will happen to you out here."

Just then, the humming of the motor became quiet, and Leslie felt the boat slow down. She started to hear something in the distance, and as they get closer, she recognized that it was the sound of water gently colliding against rocks. As the boat continued to slow, the thick fog began to disappear. She was then presented with the image of a dock in the distance, with an older gentleman standing there waving excitedly.

The man had dark olive skin and a long, thick salt-and-pepper beard, more salt than pepper. The color of his curly hair matched his beard. The professor removed his gloves, took off his big round garden hat, and gave a slight bow to Leslie.

As they all disembarked, one by one, they greeted the man like an old friend. Ori said, "Professor Raziel, I'd like to introduce you to —"

"Leslie," Professor Raziel said, finishing Ori's sentence. "Yes, welcome, welcome, welcome. I'm so happy to have you here finally. Please come inside. I'm sure you've had a rough day or two and can use a hot meal and some rest."

As they walked up the dock toward the inland part of the island, Leslie looked around and saw nothing but large, thick trees. The woods seemed so dense that she wondered how much it must have cost to build any type of structure on this island. Once they got closer to the trees, the shade from the canopy covered Leslie. The group headed down a narrow path that got wider as they walked deeper into the woods. Suddenly, the trail opened up to beautiful gardens with fruits, vegetables, herbs, and flowers. The entire space seemed to be in the shape of a massive circle running parallel to the tree line. The open area was at least ten acres in size. The well-manicured garden reminded Leslie of something one might see in palatial gardens in

France or Spain. The vibrant colors of the garden and the way the trail subtly vanished back into the woods reminded Leslie of the painting *The Artist's Garden at Giverny* by Claude Monet.

At a midpoint in the garden was an exquisite stone construct that resembled something built in the twelfth or thirteenth centuries. As they continued toward the house while engaged in casual chatter, Leslie stared at the rows of fruit and noticed the plums that looked perfectly ripe.

"Would you like to try one? They've been delicious this year," Professor Raziel asked as he picked one off the tree.

Leslie graciously accepted the fruit. She savored the sweet and tangy fruit, the juice running down her fingers, as they continued walking toward the house.

The true centerpiece of the open acreage was a house made of elegantly crafted marble and limestone. The dirt trail stopped at the entranceway. The front door was a beautiful dark wood bound with iron. The window frames and other features were surprisingly modern for a house in the middle of a forest on an island. As Leslie stood on the front stoop, looking up at the two-story construct, the house seemed much larger than she initially thought.

"This place is massive," Leslie said.

"Just wait until you get inside," Ori responded.

Chapter 24

Inside, Leslie was surprised by how bright the space felt. There was a giant circular skylight in the center of the roof, allowing plenty of natural light to brighten the marble building.

"Leslie," Professor Raziel interrupted her thoughts, "is everything alright? What am I saying? Of course, it's not," he answered himself. "You've had quite a hectic turn of events."

"I'm sorry. I'm just taking all of this in," Leslie said. "What a lovely and unexpected surprise."

"Take your time," Ori said. "It can be overwhelming at first."

"I'm sure all of you are hungry," the professor said. "Leslie, please feel free to do some exploring, and once you are ready, we will have a nice warm meal ready for you. Please don't feel rushed and try to get some rest. You are safe here."

The color inside the house came from an amazing collection of art pieces. The walls of the first floor were covered by works of Salvador Dalí, Frida Kahlo, Pablo Picasso, and René Magritte.

"Is this Dalí's *The Persistence of Memory*?" Leslie asked, amazed.

"Why, yes, it is," the professor said. "Are you an art fan?"

"Sort of. I took a class on art history while studying abroad in Spain during college. That was my introduction to surrealism," Leslie said.

"Lovely. I find all forms of art interesting. My favorite, as you can tell, are works in which the artist tries to depict dreams."

Leslie tried to suppress a yawn.

The professor gave her an understanding look and said, "You'll be staying in a room upstairs. There's a bathroom in there where you can get cleaned up. There are some clothes in the room that should fit you as well."

"I'll show you the way," Ori said.

The work on the walls along the stairwell as well as on the second floor were pieces Leslie didn't recognize. They were even more vibrant and captivating. "What are these?" Leslie asked.

"These are works by different indigenous tribes around the world. Some cultures believe that shapes are the best way to depict dreams, the universe, and even the creator." Ori explained the geometric style being represented in a particular painting. He then opened a door at the top of the stairs. "This is your room. The bathroom has a nice shower, and clothes are in the chest of drawers."

After Leslie showered, she went through the clothes in the drawers and realized that they did, in fact, fit her. She wondered if this was someone's room. There weren't any photos on display. No way it was Jordan's room; she was too small to fit these clothes. The room mainly consisted of bookshelves full of books. Leslie saw a mix of classics, such as *Sense and Sensibility* and *Pride and Prejudice*, as well as some mysteries by authors like Agatha Christie.

Leslie made her way downstairs and noticed a massive bookcase that stood around seven feet high, with rows and rows of books covering an entire wall of the house. She looked for a clock to get some sense of time. She never wore a watch, and she had given her phone to Tony before the flight. Then she heard the professor's voice coming from the distance. "Feeling better, Leslie?"

"Yes! There's something transformative about a nice, hot shower," she responded.

"I'm working on supper now," the professor said.

"Thank you," she replied. After a pause, she commented, "I wasn't expecting there to be so much natural light in here with all of these trees."

"I have a wonderful architect," Professor Raziel said. "I try to get as much natural light as I can during the day to prevent me from straining my eyes as I read."

Leslie started to stroll by the books on the shelves that bordered the walls. "Some of these books seem extremely old," she said, stopping to look at leather-bound editions.

"I'm a bit of a collector," Professor Raziel admitted. "I love knowing as much as I can about everything. The ones I keep in the living room are my favorites, and I refer to them most often. You'd be surprised how much information gets lost with every new edition of a book. So, I make it a point to keep as many original copies as possible."

"It's good to see that people are still drawn to books," the professor continued. The professor walked to one section. "This is my religion section. Here I keep what I believe are the most significant and widely accepted religious texts." The professor ran his fingers along the texts. "You have various versions of the Bible, of course, the Torah, the Qur'an. Oh, the Vedas, the Tao Te Ching, *The Egyptian Book of the Dead*." The professor looked over at Leslie. "I also have Upanishads, Buddhist sutras, you know, the list goes on.

"I also have religious texts that aren't so widely accepted or distributed. Then I begin to move to more philosophical texts. Here is the *Book of Enoch*, the works of Plato. If you continue moving to the right," the professor said, "you'll start to get into the diaries of some of the greatest minds that have ever existed."

"Are these Leonardo da Vinci's notebooks?" Leslie exclaimed.

The professor moved to her side. "Why, yes, they are, but those are in Italian. If you want, I can pull the English translations from the cellar."

"No, no, that's okay," Leslie said, completely shocked that either was even an option.

"Next, we get into wars throughout history, starting back to Mesopotamia 2300 BC." The professor proudly showed off his books. Just then, Tony walked in, went to the very end of the shelves, and pulled out a couple of skinny books. "And at the end," the professor said with a goofy grin, "I keep my favorite comics."

"Put them back when you are finished, please," the professor said to Tony as if talking to a stubborn teenager.

"I will," said Tony as he walked outside to sit on the back deck.

"You always say you will, and you never do," the professor called after him, smiling as Tony closed the door behind him.

"You have an incredible library," Leslie said with admiration.

"This is just the tip of the iceberg," the professor said as he guided her into the living room. "Anyone who is a guest here can read any book. Most of these are the main writings of commonly accepted ideas and literature. All except this one," said the professor as he pulled one book from the shelf. It was a thick, black, leather-bound book.

"There's no title," Leslie said.

"That is correct. But it is a book that covers the history of Lilith and Adam, and it is one of the rarest books in the collection. I would keep it downstairs, but I've been referring to it so often lately that I needed to move it up from my archives."

"I've never heard of The history of Lilith and Adam," Leslie said as she gingerly thumbed the pages of the old book. "What material are these pages made of?"

"Ah," the professor said, "that's hemp. If you are ever back here, I will encourage you to explore more of my library. I have many wonderful, obscure texts that will transcend you to another world," the professor said with a smile on his face. "Please sit tight, I have water on the stove. I'll bring you some tea."

"That would be wonderful, thank you," Leslie said with a smile. She selected a book and settled into an amazingly cozy couch.

Chapter 25

Leslie awoke with the book on the floor beside her and a full, untouched cup of tea on the side table. She heard the sounds of a lively discussion coming from outside.

She walked toward the open French doors to get a better view. Jordan, Professor Raziel, Tony, and Ori were all sitting around a dining table on the beautiful back deck, seemingly midway through what looked to be a delicious dinner.

She hadn't been spotted yet, and she could hear Tony trying his best to keep his voice down. "But do you think she's ready?"

Tony was looking at the professor, who replied, "It's not up to me, and you know that."

"She's ready," Ori said. "She has to be. Jordan will be there for her."

"Leslie," Jordan said for the benefit of the group. "Please join us."

Leslie collected herself before stepping out to join them at the table. "Sorry about that," Leslie said. "I didn't mean to eavesdrop."

"I'm sure you want to know what's going on, and you have that right since you are now involved in this." Ori looked to the professor. "Would you mind?"

"Leslie, let me tell you a story about a boy I met. From birth, everyone knew he was pretty special. They say that when he was born, he didn't start crying immediately. His eyes wandered around taking things in, and he only started crying once parted from his mother. Once older, he was an exceptional student. I came across him when he was a teenager, studying advanced physics and catching the attention of his elders."

"Did you go to college early?" Leslie asked Ori, as she started helping herself to some food.

"Nah, I kept hanging around these knuckleheads," Ori said with a wink.

"It was obvious that he was eager to learn, so I took Ori under my wing and started giving him new works to study. He soaked up the knowledge incredibly quickly." The professor gave Leslie a knowing look. "Of course, you can imagine that before long he was thinking about ways to apply the knowledge and was considering what changes he could make."

"What kind of books were you giving him?" Leslie nudged the professor playfully.

"Professor Raziel was a bit of a secret hippie," Ori teased.

"I loved teaching future leaders, artists, musicians, historians, innovators. And that path led me to mentor this young man. When I realized how brilliant Ori was, I made an agreement with his mother to act as his personal tutor."

"So Ori had an apprenticeship?" Leslie said.

"Yes, you could think of it like that," the professor smiled. "Apprenticeships are so uncommon these days. So I created a tailored curriculum for him that was meant to last two years. Ori plowed through it all in two months."

"Is that true?" Leslie asked, surprised.

"Well, the professor wasn't exactly clear on the timeline, so I thought it was all summer reading," Ori said.

"As he read more books," the professor continued, "and gained more knowledge, he told me he realized what he was meant to do." The professor looked over at Ori. "Do you remember what you said?"

"Of course I do," Ori said. "I want to be able to help as many people as possible live a life full of joy."

"But we also realized," the professor said, "there would most likely be people who would be against that."

"Why would you think that?" Leslie asked.

"Because his plan was going to cause some powerful people to make less money. But it was the only conceivable way to allow more people to get out of debt, earn a good living, and take care of their families," Professor Raziel said.

Ori joined in with a bleak tone that Leslie has never heard him use before. "Something big is coming. The wedges that we've built could continue to divide us until people just give up. And giving up will be the end of life as we know it."

Looking fatigued, Ori walked back into the house, and the professor continued, "You have to understand what the aim has been for Ori. He believes that it is vital to give people something to care for, something to hang onto for dear life. In the beginning, when tribes could not sustain more than a hundred and fifty people, everyone shared in the knowledge and worked to help the entire population succeed. Since modern farming and expansion, civilizations have become more focused on controlling as much land and as many people as possible for the benefit of a few. It was never really fair, but it has gotten progressively worse over time. There has, of course, been progress in personal and religious freedoms, but there is still a long way to go. What Ori aimed to do was work on tackling what he believed was the next major shackle holding the masses down: financial freedom. People are strapped down with debt, having trouble getting ahead, while seeing a few who have everything."

The professor sat back and continued, "If people don't feel like they have anything of value worth fighting for, then why fight at all?"

"People fight to survive," Leslie said with conviction.

"But what's considered surviving? Constantly being stressed because you don't know if you will be able to afford the rent or pay your medical bills? Always worrying that your child may not come home from school?" The professor took a deep breath. "What would you say if I could offer you an alternative?"

"It depends on the alternative," Leslie said.

"A world with financial freedom. A peaceful world. No more war. No more prejudice. No more hate. What would you say to that?"

"I would ask, what's the catch?" Leslie said.

The professor smiled. "That's the correct response." He stood up and picked up his plate. Jordan and Tony, previously silent observers of this conversation, stood up and followed his lead, cleaning off the table.

"I think that we've had a busy couple of days. You should get some more rest," the professor said to Leslie.

Leslie made her way back upstairs. She started to get settled in for the night and noticed one of the professor's ancient, leather-bound books on the nightstand. It was the book that contained the history of Lilith and Adam. Leslie attempted to read the book, but her fatigue got the best of her, and she fell asleep immediately.

Chapter 26

Leslie opened her eyes, hearing voices that sounded far away. She must have been incredibly tired; she didn't even remember falling asleep. She rubbed her eyes and stretched under the soft sheets, then finally pulled herself up to a sitting position. The sun peeked through the blinds, creating a glow against the gold curtains. As she looked around, reacquainting herself with the room, she took note of the clock hanging on the far wall. It was a beautiful antique wooden clock with a white and gold face and what appeared to be a small colorful landscape painted at the base. She was marveling again at how incredible this house was when she realized that the clock read almost ten in the morning.

She heard the voices again, recognizing them as Tony's and Ori's, and decided to join them. She threw on more clothes and then went to grab the book off the nightstand, but it wasn't there. She ran her hand over the sheets but didn't find it there either. Weird, she thought. But maybe

Jordan had looked in on her last night and then put the book back in the library.

Leslie opened the door to head downstairs and heard Tony say, "Good luck, and I hope you know what you are doing."

"Trust me," Leslie heard Ori reply.

"What if something goes wrong?" Tony asked.

"Nothing will go wrong," Ori replied. "Now get out of here; you've got work to do. I'll catch up with you when I can."

Leslie arrived downstairs at the same time as the front door closed. "Where did Tony go?" she asked.

"He had some things that he needed to take care of," Ori said. "He'll be back before long."

As Leslie walked toward the kitchen, she said, "Please tell me there's coffee."

Ori held up the pot, smiled, and said, "You know it." He poured her a cup. "You like it black, right? One teaspoon of sugar?"

"What self-respecting, criminal mastermind makes other people coffee?" Leslie asked him with a smile.

"Wow, okay," said Ori. "I see you're feeling better."

Leslie laughed and took the cup of coffee from him. She exhaled deeply as she took a sip, and then said, "You're a good man, Ori."

"There are some biscuits and fresh jam on the table if you're hungry," she heard Professor Raziel say as he entered the house with a basket full of carrots, potatoes, and yellow onions, all still covered with fertile black soil from the garden.

Leslie helped herself to a fluffy biscuit, spreading some butter and jam on it, when Ori walked over and asked, "Would you mind taking a walk with me? There's something I'd like to discuss with you."

As the two started their stroll, Leslie mirrored Ori's leisurely pace. His arms were comfortably resting behind his back, with one hand lightly grasping the opposite wrist. As she enjoyed the delicious biscuit, he stopped here and there to explore plants growing in the garden. He looked like he didn't have a care in the world.

"Man, I love this place," Ori said as he gently ran a cupped hand along one of the shrubs. He placed his hand close to his nose, inhaled deeply, and then smiled, "and the smell of rosemary."

"What is this place?" Leslie asked. "I mean, I know that we were en route to Canada, but I've never heard of a place quite like this in the Pacific Northwest."

"This is an ancient botanical garden of sorts. It's very private, and few people have membership access. It's a place where I love to come and recharge my batteries. Here, I can escape all of the daily distractions that throw my energy out of whack." Ori looked over to Leslie. "You know?"

"I hear you. This place is amazing." Leslie nodded.

"The professor has coined this place The Point of Singularity. It's actually where I got the name for the company."

Leslie closed her eyes and inhaled deeply. As she exhaled, the events of late flashed by. She looked over to Ori. "Is everything going to be okay?" Leslie tried to read his face. "I trust you, but I'm still not really sure what's going on."

"You're tough, and we're working toward making everything okay," Ori said, maintaining a calm expression. "I know these are unique circumstances. After this, you're going to have a whole new threshold for worry."

They both let out a small laugh.

The pair walked down a path at the back of the house. This trail started wide and grew narrow as it wound deeper into the woods. After nearly one hundred meters of following the trail, which was surrounded by thick green shrubs and trees, the path opened up to a field of lavender. They walked to the edge of the field, and Leslie realized that it was actually a cliff, overlooking a beautiful, wide valley.

Ori asked, "Do you see the tree line at the far edge of the valley?"

"Yes," Leslie responded, nodding.

"What would you say if I told you that somewhere past that tree line you could find every living creature known to man, and maybe more?" Ori asked.

"I would say that's kind of hard to imagine, Noah," Leslie responded, amusing herself. The stress had made her a little more sarcastic than normal.

Ori laughed and exclaimed, "Our imaginations are too limited!"

"Tell me again, why did you come work for Singularity?" Ori asked after a short pause, looking out across the valley.

"Well, I believe in what you stand for. I believe in what the company represents," Leslie said.

Ori studied her intently, remaining quiet.

Leslie continued, impassioned, "You use your company to help people stand up on their own. Your business is the first I've encountered where you consistently do right by your employees first, then your customers. I guess not having shareholders allows you a certain level of freedom, but more than that, you try and fix problems that other companies and people in power choose to ignore."

After considering this, Ori said, "One of my favorite subjects to study is history. I think that history is one of the most important aspects of civilization that we can examine, not necessarily the history that is taught in school, but what actually happened. Then you will be empowered to alter the future." Ori frowned, "I'm afraid that if things don't change drastically, then our future—the world's future— will be bleak. One of the reasons I created this company was because I saw again and again throughout history what happens when the majority have nothing and the minority have everything."

Ori paused before continuing. "Our efforts to change that have made us a target. Even if we resolve this, history tells us that people in my position don't tend to make it out unscathed. I'd like you to be my successor."

"What are you talking about? There has to be someone other than me. I mean," Leslie stammered, caught completely off guard, "I'll be happy to run the executive search to find the ideal replacement. But I don't think that I'm capable of — "

"Enough," Ori interrupted her rambling. "What makes you think that you are not capable? Better yet, it does not matter because whatever it is, you are wrong. Ignore all the noise telling you that you can't do anything. You can do everything you put your heart and soul into." Locking eyes with Leslie, he asked again, "Will you be the next leader?"

"Umm, of course, I'd be honored to," Leslie found herself saying, feeling a blend of pride and sadness rising in her chest.

"Now don't get too emotional; I'm pretty sure I can find a way out of this dilemma. But when I do, I still want you to take over for me," Ori said with a smile.

"What?" Leslie said. "Why? If you're around, then I think you should lead the company."

"You're going to be great. You'll have Roger and Jordan by your side. You believe in the mission of the company, and I know that you will protect that. And when I get to the other side of this, there are other things that I need to look after." Ori clasped his arms behind his back again. "This has been in my plans for a while. I needed to find a suitable replacement so that I could continue with my mission. Starting and running the Singularity Group was a small but important piece of a bigger, complex puzzle. It's time for me to move on." There was something so final about the way he said that.

They both looked off into the distance for a while, admiring the way that the midday sun shone on the valley. "Thank you for everything," Leslie finally said. It was all she could manage.

Chapter 27

Ori and Leslie heard soft footprints approaching. They turned to see Professor Raziel. "Leslie," Ori said, "will you excuse me? I need to take care of some things."

"Of course," Leslie said, and she then shifted her gaze to the professor. "Hey."

"Beautiful, isn't it?" asked the professor. Leslie nodded her head in agreement and let the moment become quiet again as they appreciated the view.

Something told her that the professor knew what Ori brought her out here to discuss. So after a few moments, she confessed, "I don't know if I can do it. I can't be him."

"Of course not," Professor Raziel said simply. "Your task isn't to be like Ori and do things the way that Ori did. Your job is to do things the way that Leslie would do them. Trust yourself; we do."

"How are you so confident? We've just met," Leslie said.

"You and I may have just met, but I know much more about you than you think," he said as he glanced over in her direction. "I know about your parents' and grandparents' shining legal careers, which inspired your own."

Leslie said, "Well, yes." She then waited to see what he had to say next.

Professor Raziel looked like he was gauging how much to say, then continued, "I also know that when you were fifteen, you had a friend who was three years older than you who got in with the wrong crowd. She was arrested for selling drugs."

"Allegedly," Leslie interrupted as if she were currently defending her friend. Then with a tentative smile, she added, "And what did your research say about that?"

Professor Raziel said, "I know that you got your friend out of trouble without your family finding out. Your friend had a public defender with very little experience to speak of. You fed this attorney an extremely well-crafted argument, with pictures, cue cards, and highlighted legal precedents. That was the first criminal defense case that guy ever won."

Leslie realized her mouth was ajar. That was not what she expected him to say, and she had to work to collect herself. Professor Raziel continued, "I particularly liked the legend that you created for him. What was it, lines that were highlighted using a pink marker were anticipated rebuttals and lines highlighted in green markers were key points that would put the prosecution on their heels? Your empathy is an asset; never underestimate its importance. What made you so driven to help her?"

"She was a friend of mine, like family," Leslie said.

The professor watched her face, and after a moment probed, "There was more, wasn't there?"

"She had a good heart." Leslie sighed. "I'd known her since middle school. She lived in the apartment complex down the street. We walked to school together every day. Not many people knew that she had a disability, and she was very trusting. Some people saw that she was easy to influence and manipulate and took advantage of her," Leslie said, shaking her head. "She was pretty, and in my neighborhood, it was common for older guys to use silly young girls. I feared the court system would not fairly account for her mental disability, and I couldn't let a person like that get caught up in the criminal system. I had to do something."

Professor Raziel nodded, looking as she had just confirmed what he already knew.

Leslie didn't expect a straight answer, but had to ask, "How did you know all of that? I never told a soul, and that public defender would never have opened his mouth to give the credit to someone else."

"Part of my role is to hear all and know all," Professor Raziel said evasively, with a broad smile pointed in her direction. Then with a more serious tone, he said, "Leslie, you did the right thing by your friend. You constantly do the right thing. That's why Ori chose you. If you continue just as you have been, you will surprise yourself."

After a few moments in silence, Professor Raziel looked at Leslie again as he started to turn back toward the path. "Ready to head back?"

Chapter 28

"Okay," Jordan said. "It took me longer than I anticipated, but here's everything I could find on Silas. Someone did an impressive job trying to erase the guy's military history."

"Anything that jumps out at you?" Ori asked.

"Actually," Jordan's fingers flew across her keyboard, "since someone tried so hard to erase his military record, that piqued my interest first." Jordan landed on the file that she was searching for. "I think that it has something to do with this note. I found a single message between two very senior political advisors at that time saying that they believed they had found the next person to run the program."

"What program?" Tony asked as he walked back into the house.

"That wasn't exactly clear, and both of those men have had untimely deaths since that message was sent. But, I did some digging in their backgrounds, and both of them have ties to COINTELPRO."

The professor's head shot up. "COINTELPRO?"

Everyone looked at him, now very curious as to what he had to share.

The professor saw their faces, took a breath, and prepared to teach. "In the mid-1950s, the FBI started a program focused on disrupting activities thought to be orchestrated by the Communist Party. In the 1960s, the program shifted its attention to other domestic groups that were thought to be subversive or to any group that could disrupt the existing social and political order. The program was run by William Sullivan, who was tapped by J. Edgar Hoover himself."

"Wasn't Sullivan the guy who put wiretaps on Martin Luther King Jr.'s phones?" Leslie asked.

"Exactly," the professor responded. "In the late 1970s, there was a Congressional House Select Committee set up to investigate the assassinations of civil rights leaders, and just days before Sullivan was supposed to testify, he was killed in a hunting accident."

"Wait, I remember reading about this program. According to what I read, COINTELPRO was targeting militant groups like the KKK, the Communist Party, and the Black Panthers," Leslie said.

"Well, that's what was revealed to the public. Their main focus was on any person or organization that might disrupt the social order that was in place. In order for COINTELPRO to take action, those persons or organizations needed to appear to be a danger to the system. They were known to make anyone who wouldn't conform to their ideals appear to be a violent threat."

The professor shook his head. "The program was supposedly shut down in 1971, but there were rumors that the more extremist members found some very wealthy and powerful donors and continued the initiative in the shadows."

"That tracks," Tony chimed in. "If they have roots in the FBI and access to funding by some of the elites in this country, they could have a hand in this."

"I don't understand why they would be coming after you, Ori. It's not like you are a political activist," Leslie said.

The professor answered. "Ori isn't talking about change; he's making it. And while he's doing it, he's contradicting all of the theories that have been used to oppress people for generations. This could make mainstream America start to question everything. Think about it. In America, we're told that sixty-eight percent of prisoners released from prison commit a crime and return within three years. And that message is pushed out into the world without the bigger picture. Leslie, how long has the prisoner work program been running?"

"It's going on its eighth year," Leslie replied.

"And of the two thousand individuals who have come through the program, how many employees have returned to prison?"

"None," Leslie replied.

"Exactly, this program is showing what people in other countries have long ago determined. Many people make stupid mistakes when they are young. If you don't strip them of their humanity and, instead, give them a chance for true rehabilitation and a shot at establishing a good life, they aren't likely to return to prison."

The group is silent as they process what the professor just said.

The professor continued, "Having people question what the authorities say is one thing, but I would also imagine that what's frustrating them is that Ori is also impacting their money.

"What are you talking about?" Leslie asked.

"Ori's business model is proving that you can sacrifice margin in the short term, pay people great wages, and still continue to see your business grow and be very competitive. People who work within your network are financially independent, and in return, they are more loyal, which makes your business grow even more. This is great for you, your employees, and society, but the masters don't own it. Ori is going around the system and making changes to it without their permission. He's uncontrollable, and he's not at the table with them."

"I've been asked countless times to go public, of course, but we don't need to. Plus, I'm afraid that if we go public, the focus will be on paying more to the investors and offering less to our employees, customers, and partners. We would be in that vicious cycle of cost-cutting and layoffs every three months so the company's shareholders can get the financial returns they think they deserve," Ori said.

"I know all too well," said the professor. "They have probably been hoping you would be lured in by the possibility of incredible wealth and give up true ownership of your company to the market. Then they could vote you out over time and slowly destroy what you've built."

Tony spoke up with a look of certainty on his face, "They had a plan for you. If you hadn't taken the Wesley Corporation bait, they would have taken you out in a loud way. They'd say that you were at war with the most notorious crime syndicate and that the Wesley Corporation deal was an aggressive move on their territory and was also the final straw. They'd damage your legacy, remove you from the picture, and then work to systematically break apart everything that you've been creating."

"Alright, so if we assume that this secret social oppression government agency is up and running in the shadows, and if we think that this Silas guy is running the program, then what next?" Leslie asked. "I mean, we can't turn him in without any proof. Plus, who would listen to us?"

"It wouldn't matter if we caught him. It wouldn't matter if we turned him in and if he spent the rest of his life in prison. These things are set up so that all liability would lie with him. Once he's gone, then they will simply find someone else to fill that seat. And he knows what he signed up for," Tony said.

"Who we are going after is the person who decides the next person to fill that seat. The handler's handler," Ori said. "And we're going to take his power away from him."

Ori sifts through the stack of documents that make up Silas's files and picks up a picture with his Special Forces unit. It was a diverse group of guys. Ori looked at Jordan and said, "Something isn't right. Can you look into what happened to his former unit? A man who leads a unit like this isn't the same man who would knowingly run a program with the goal of social oppression."

"Every member of his old unit is deceased," Jordan said.

"All of them?" Tony asked with surprise.

"Yes, they were killed during a covert mission. A lot of the details are redacted," Jordan said.

"Do you think this is what drove Silas to take on a new position?" Leslie asked.

Jordan shook her head and said, "It looks like Silas took his new position before that mission."

"What is Silas's last known address?" Ori asked.

"Somewhere in Virginia, I'll work on the details."

"Great. And find out everything you can about the last mission of his former unit. Who sanctioned it? What was the purpose? Who was the target? Everything." Ori turned to Tony. "Are you up for a trip to our nation's capital?"

Chapter 29

Ori's phone buzzed. He looked down and saw that he had an incoming call. He answered the phone call and heard a familiar voice.

"How are you, my friend?" Carlos asked.

"It's been a while, Carlos. How are you?" Ori replied.

"Well enough. I see that your business is doing very well. Congratulations," Carlos said. "I've always wanted to see you do great things."

"Thank you, it's been a journey," Ori said. "So, to what do I owe the pleasure?"

"Yes, well, right to it then. I've heard that you have come into some grave trouble lately," Carlos said. "I fear that you are being used as a pawn to come after me."

"What makes you think that?" Ori asked.

"Well, let me ask you this, are you planning on entering the same . . .," Carlos paused, searching for the right words, "business ventures that I'm allegedly involved in?"

"Of course not," Ori said simply, without hesitation.

"I have ears everywhere, and the information that's getting whispered back to me is that there is a new competitor in town who is trying to start a war with me. Have you heard about what they've done to some very tenured people in my organization?" Carlos's tone darkened.

"I have heard a little about it. It's pretty gruesome," Ori said.

"Now, we know that you do not have that in you," Carlos continued, "and no one else has claimed ownership. In my world, if someone is going to make such a loud statement, it does not take long before he reveals who he is. I've come to believe that I have a business partnership that has clearly come to an end."

After a moment, Ori asked, "Did you hear that I met with the Wesley brothers?"

"Interestingly enough, I did hear that you met with them and that you intended to acquire the company, and then I heard about your car. Though a Cadillac did not sound quite your speed." Carlos said with a chuckle. "I'm glad you aren't hurt, my friend. And I have trust that you saw the writing on the walls."

"I didn't know exactly what was going on, but I knew it didn't feel right. Was my car a friendly notice to think twice?" Ori asked.

"I hate that you have to ask, but I suppose that's a fair question. No is the answer. That's what this call was intended to be," Carlos replied.

"I only ask because there was a man with the Wesley brothers who reminded me of a kid from the soccer team you sponsored years ago. I believe Nicolas was his name," Ori said.

Carlos was silent for more than a few seconds "Yes, Nicolas. Someone is playing a very dangerous game with both of us. I'm afraid that this poor, misguided soul is unwittingly caught in the middle."

Ori sighed. "I don't know if I can end this before he reaches the point of no return."

"That burden is not on you. That is poor Nicolas's decision. Ori, remember, your task isn't to save everyone, just to save those who choose to be saved." Carlos continued, "Well, it's always a pleasure. I must go now. Know this, you don't have to worry about my people or me. We have made a covenant and will honor it. Let me know if I can be of any assistance."

"I appreciate it, Carlos. Take care," Ori said and then hung up the phone.

Chapter 30

Silas sat in his car patiently, observing the windshield fog up from the combination of his breathing and the temperature outside. As he cracked his window, the passenger side of his car opened, and Nicolas climbed into the vehicle. Nicolas and Silas were parked in an abandoned shopping mall parking lot just outside of the Atlanta metro area.

Nicolas was the first to speak. "What in the world am I doing out here? You said that we shouldn't meet in person again."

"Must you always complain about something?" Silas asked. "Listen, it's time for you to do your job."

"What are you talking about? I've been doing my job," Nicolas shot back. Silas remained silent, with a stone-cold facial expression, his eyes drilling a hole through Nicolas.

Nicolas's smile slowly fades from his face as he stammers "a . . . are you serious? Now? After all this time?"

Silas turned his head to look out the windshield, focusing his eyes on the grass that was growing out of a small crack in the concrete. "They're on to her. We think Ori knows she has been up to something."

"Does he know who she is or who we are?" Nicolas asked.

"You mean, does Ori know that you are on the run from the most dangerous cartel on the planet and that you made the cartel boss's only daughter try to entrap him?" Silas looked over again. "I don't think so. But . . ." Silas paused. "That's why you need to do your job before Ori finds all that out. Or worse, before Daddy Devil finds out."

"I mean," Nicolas shifts in his seat and lets out a nervous chuckle, "it's been five years. I—"

Silas cuts him short. "I told you how this most likely would end. I told you not to get attached. Grab the bag."

Nicolas lowered his eyes, slowly turned to face the back seats and grabbed a black backpack. As he began to face forward, Silas grabbed him by his neck and shoved his face hard against the side of the passenger seat. Nicolas tried to fight free but was no match for Silas's strength. Silas leaned in, and through clenched teeth said, "Listen very closely. I want to remind you of some things. I'm sure you're considering not doing what's been asked of you, and you're desperately trying to think of a way to get out of this crappy situation that you've gotten yourself into. Well, I'm here to tell you, there's no easy way out of this one."

Nicolas stopped resisting, and Silas continued, "You screwed up, and we got you. You were nothing, and we could have let you be slaughtered by your boss, but we kept you alive. We allowed you to be someone else, to pretend you aren't the coward we all know you to be. We made you successful. We put you and that girl together. We told you that as long as you both stayed useful, then we would continue to protect you. And you agreed that if she ever became a liability, then you would take care of her, or we would take care of both of you. Or worse, stop protecting and hiding both of you. So, the ball is in your court, Nicolas."

Silas slowly released Nicolas's neck and faced forward again, locking his gaze back on the blades of grass bending in the wind. Nicolas looked down like a defeated dog, holding the bag in his lap.

Silas added, "I shouldn't have to tell you this, but make sure it looks like she offed herself. Now get out of my car."

Nicolas grabbed the bag and stepped out of the car. As he walked quickly away, Silas called after him, "Oh, and get it over quickly. This thing doesn't need to drag on. As soon as I get confirmation that she's no longer breathing, I will work on getting approval to move you."

Chapter 31

"Hey, hey, hey," Mikiko said to catch Evelyn's attention as Evelyn jumped up from her computer with excitement, holding a scrap of paper in her hand. Still, on the telephone, Mikiko said, "Okay, thank you."

"What's up?" Evelyn asked as Mikiko hung up the phone.

"Monica Nichols has been missing all week. A team just went to her place and found blood everywhere."

"Did they get the blood to the lab?" Evelyn asked.

"They did, and it came back as a positive match for Monica's DNA. The more interesting part is that the DNA was put through our global database, and there was an exact match for someone else in the system."

"A twin?" Agent Cramer asked as he joined the conversation.

"No, my contact in the forensics unit just sent the file over."

"Even a twin wouldn't have an exact match," Evelyn said as she hurried over to the computer screen to see the online report file.

"The report came back for a Jackeline Gutierrez de la Cruz," Mikiko said. "Her blood samples were in the system because of an eye procedure that she had when she was a child."

"Where does she come from?" Cramer asked.

"It looks like she's from Central America, but she somehow attended the Institut Le Rosey in Switzerland, only the most prestigious boarding school in the world at the low, low price of a hundred and fifty grand per year," Mikiko said.

Evelyn asked, "No records on her parents?"

"Just her mom. It looks like her mom owned a restaurant in a small town. No record for the dad. Separately, I have another couple of anomalies to look into further," Mikiko said. "After reviewing the security footage and visitor logs for the weeks before and after the explosion, I decided to cross-reference everyone's digital histories." Mikiko clicked on a file. "Two people stood out, and they visited at the same time right before the explosion."

"The suspense is killing me," Appleton said, having walked up while Mikiko was talking. "Please get on with it."

"Both of them were members of the Wesley Corporation's deal team. One was a man named Silas

Stillman. He has a military background, and I tried to pull his military record, but the files were blocked. The other was a man by the name of Nicolas Villalobos."

"What were you able to find on him?" Evelyn asked.

"Nothing yet, but I'm still working it," Mikiko said, discreetly glancing toward the section chief.

"Got it. Keep working it, and hopefully we can get a good lead," Evelyn replied.

"Agent Shikibu, didn't you just say that this Monica Nichols was also using a fake alias?" Appleton said.

"Yes, sir."

"And why didn't she come up in your data search?" Appleton asked, his voice dripping in condescension.

"She did, sir, I just —" Mikiko tried to say, but Appleton cut her off.

"How can we trust any of this data that you are providing? It doesn't seem all that precise, now does it? Ladies, you're not living up to your reputations." He then quickly turned to Agent Cramer and said, "You and Agent Chivington, meet me in my office."

"Agent Cramer," Evelyn jumped in, refusing to be deterred, "what did you find on the cell phones that you recovered from the plane? Anything from that unread message?"

The men all stare at Evelyn for a few seconds without saying a word. "Well?" Evelyn pressed. "Did you find anything that could help?"

Appleton looked at Agent Cramer and nodded his head in the direction of Evelyn. Agent Cramer walked to his desk, retrieving Ori's phone. "The unread message was a large series of random numbers; we're taking it to be decoded," he said as he handed it to Evelyn.

"I guess we are okay getting fingerprints all over evidence now," Evelyn said as she pulled out a rubber glove from her pocket to grab the phone from Agent Cramer. Before Cramer could respond, Evelyn continued, "How large was the data set of random numbers?"

"About two hundred fifty numbers. Take a look at it yourself."

Evelyn turned the phone on, quickly accessed the message, and within a few seconds, started to laugh.

"What's funny, Agent Blackwood?" Appleton asked.

"This is just binary code. And I'm pretty sure Ori meant for us to find this message."

"Well then what does it say?" Cramer asked.

Evelyn translated it quickly. "Not yet, but we will meet soon." She looked up at the men. "He's having a little fun with us."

The men kept watching Evelyn, clearly trying to decide what to do next.

Evelyn broke the silence. "It's a gift. We will keep reviewing the information that Mikiko has been going over. Didn't you gentlemen have something you needed to discuss in private?"

As the men left the room, Evelyn turned back to Mikiko. "Okay, what did you really find, and why did you hide it?"

"That's my girl," Mikiko said with a smile. "Okay, after I got Nicolas's name, I ran his face through the NSA's global system and found this," Mikiko said as she pulled up a picture of Nicolas. "This is Nicolas."

"Got it," Evelyn confirmed.

"Now check this out. I found another photo of him," Mikiko said as she pulled up a picture of Nicolas with Monica Nichols in the upper corner of her screen on an amusement park ride.

"When was this picture taken?" Evelyn asked.

"Over three years ago. The photo was posted online by someone else on the ride. I would imagine that Monica and Nicolas didn't realize that it existed. They have otherwise both done a really good job of staying off the grid."

"So there's definitely a link between the two," Evelyn said. "Why didn't you want to share this with the rest of the team?"

"Agent Chivington and Cramer were both running through the list of visitors in and out of the company, and I was doing background checks on the employees. After I found this photo, I did a bit more digging into Nicolas's background. I may or may not have explored some restricted files. But he was tagged as a member of La Tiniebla Cartel," Mikiko said.

"Really? That could be the link that Section Chief Appleton was looking for," Evelyn said. "He is going to love you."

"I'm not so sure about that," Mikiko said. "You see, it doesn't look like Nicolas has been active in the cartel for a while. Based on what I could find, it looks like he flipped and was in witness protection."

"Something's not adding up. Why would someone in witness protection be involved with the Wesley Corporation, especially as a member of a deal team for an opportunity this large?" Evelyn said.

"I thought the same thing," Mikiko said, "so I kept digging. You get one guess as to the agent who turned him."

"Section Chief Appleton," Evelyn said.

"Ding, ding, ding," Mikiko said.

"So, you think our team is hiding something?"

"I can't be sure, but it certainly looks questionable," Mikiko said.

"I didn't get a good feeling about it from the start," Evelyn said with a heavy sigh. "What do you have on the Wesley brothers? Any idea how Monica, or Jackeline, fits into this?"

"Nothing much there but your typical wealthy family with powerful connections. The kids seem like spoiled sociopaths, but there's nothing much there besides . . ." Mikiko paused. "How did I miss this?"

"Miss what?" Evelyn asked.

"That there's nothing there. Absolutely nothing there, and these kids are pieces of work." Mikiko began typing intensely, accessing folders and files. "There was nothing on these kids until they went to college and were living out of state. No disciplinary notes from school, no police records. The only record of bad behavior is in private messages between classmates with complaints of bullying. These kids sound cruel. Then, when they go to college, you start seeing some charges for minor drug possession and disorderly conduct. Most of those charges were eventually dropped, but the records are still there. Then once they were back in-state, nothing again. Either they changed their ways and got in line, or the local authorities are being paid to look the other way."

Mikiko continued to work her magic, fingers moving rapidly across the keyboard, eyes darting across files and pages. She pulled up a confidential file from the FBI database and breathed. "I knew it."

"What is it?" Evelyn asked.

"What do you do when the police officers in your state are corrupt and you can't get any local support? You call the FBI. And it looks like there was a nasty drug bust involving one of the sons. Some locals called the FBI, but instead of making an arrest, they converted the son into a confidential witness. The entire drug sting was completely covered up."

"I only need one guess as to who oversaw the investigation," Evelyn said as she looked over toward the section chief, who was sitting in his office with Special Agents Cramer and Chivington.

"This is big; this is huge," Mikiko said, clearly nervous as she realized the enormity of the situation. She lowered her voice instinctively. "What do we do?" They see the three men wrapping up their conversation and beginning to stand up from their seats.

"Leave it with me. Clear your entire search history. Cover your tracks," Evelyn said with urgency. "Do it quickly. I will handle this from here."

Mikiko quickly closed out of files and pulled up the geo-tracking of US airspace. "We found him. We just got a report that one of Ori's private planes reentered US airspace a few hours ago," she said just as the section chief and the other agents got back to her desk.

"Excellent, where is it heading?" Appleton asked.

Cramer had been on a brief phone call. He hung up and said, "I got confirmation that it's en route for the Washington DC area."

Appleton smiled with triumph. "Cramer, Chivington, get a plane ready to head to the capitol. Ladies, keep compiling evidence connecting this guy to the cartel." He turned to start walking away but paused briefly, turning his head to look back at the women. "And ensure it will hold up in court."

Just as the men reached the door, a faint buzzing sound started, followed by a very low chime. All of the agents reached in their pockets and pulled out their cell phones to check for new messages. One by one, they realized that the sound had come from Ori's phone on Agent Shikibu's desk. As they all move closer, the phone buzzed again followed by the faint chime. "One New Message."

Chapter 32

Mikiko looked at Evelyn. "Want to see what it says?"

"Go ahead," Evelyn replied.

Mikiko unlocked the phone. "It's binary code again. Here, I'll throw it on the large screen."

The agents looked up at the screen as Mikiko typed a string of ones and zeroes.

01001000   01100101   01101100   01101100   01101111 00001101 00001010

"Agent Shikibu, did you type that correctly?" Evelyn asked.

"I'm sure I did, but let me double-check," Mikiko responded.

Before Mikiko had a chance to validate the numbers, a second text message popped up, and she quickly typed it in as well.

01000001   01110010   01100101   00100000   01111001 01101111 01110101 00100000 01110100 01101000 01100101 01110010 01100101 00111111 00100000 00001101 00001010

"Don't worry about double-checking. I'm sure you were right. Pass me the phone," Evelyn said, and Mikiko passed her the phone.

"What do you think you are doing?" Appleton asked.

"I think that this is Ori reaching out to us. And if I'm right, this conversation is going to move quickly. The more complex the conversation, the longer the string of binary code. If there's one mistake in typing the text into the computer translator, then it could be a huge error. So I'm going to respond."

"Respond to what?" Appleton asked right as Mikiko finished inputting the first string of code into the translator.

"Well, his first message said 'Hello,' and the second message asked, 'Are you there?" Mikiko said.

"Yes, I'm here," Evelyn texted while speaking aloud for the other agents to hear her. "Who am I speaking with?"

She continued in this fashion, translating messages out loud as they came in, and then narrating as she replied.

"Who do you think?" the phone quickly responded.

"Is this Ori?" Evelyn responded.

"Yes, and who am I speaking with?"

"Agent Blackwood from the FBI."

"My apologies for keeping you waiting, I needed to get a few answers of my own."

"Prove to me that this is Ori."

There was a long pause in the room as all of the agents waited on a response. Five minutes went by, and there was still no response.

"This is a waste of time," Appleton finally said. "Alright, gentlemen, let's get the jet ready and fly to DC. We have intelligence saying that his plane has landed. And it's been confirmed that a man matching Ori's description deboarded."

Just then, there's another text message, and Evelyn began to read it to herself.

"Well," Agent Chivington said, "what does it say?"

"It's Ori." Evelyn cleared her throat. "The message references something that we saw when we were kids. We were the only ones to witness it, and we swore to keep it a secret."

"What was it?" Mikiko asked.

Evelyn shook her head. "Most people would call it the wild imaginations of a couple of kids. But this is definitely Ori."

"Confirm his location," Appleton barked.

Evelyn paused.

"That is an order, Agent Blackwood," Appleton said.

"Where are you? It's still not too late. We can offer you protection," Evelyn typed.

"I am around. We will see each other soon enough," was the reply.

"Tell him that we know he's in Virginia," Appleton said.

"You want to let him know our hand?" Mikiko asked.

"He will begin to panic, and panicked people make mistakes," Cramer said, chiming in.

"We know you are in Virginia," Evelyn said.

"Am I now? What makes you think that?"

"We have information that a plane linked to one of your many subsidiaries landed in Virginia hours ago."

"Well done. You and your team must have really done your homework. So, what next?"

"Is he taunting us?" Chivington asked, incredulous.

"It seems like it," said Cramer.

"Alright, here's what's going to happen," Appleton said. "Agent Blackwood, since you're building the rapport with this guy, you keep him engaged as long as possible. See what other clues and information you can get. Agent Shikibu and Agent Cramer, you both stay to support Agent Blackwood. Agent Chivington, you come with me to DC."

After Appleton and Chivington leave the building, one more message comes in. Evelyn paused and then told the other agents, "He says that he will be seeing us in two days and to expect to hear from him soon."

Chapter 33

Evelyn and Mikiko were anxiously waiting, staring at the phone, trying to will a new text message into existence. "What time is it?" Mikiko asked.

Evelyn checked the time on the phone. "It's about fifteen minutes before midnight. Feel free to go to sleep. I'll wake you when he makes contact."

"That's okay. I feel fine. Are you sure he's going to reach back out to us? It's been two days and we haven't heard anything," Mikiko said. Why even contact us in the first place to just leave us waiting here? He could have been free and clear but decided to — what? — toy with the FBI?"

"I'm sure that he will make contact again," replied Evelyn as she leaned back in her chair. Without noticing it, her necklace slipped out from under her blouse.

"Hey, um . . ." Mikiko said while pointing to the ring hanging at the end of the chain around Evelyn's neck.

Evelyn's eyes followed where Mikiko's finger was pointing. "Oh, thank you," she said with fatigue in her voice. "I know people like to speculate about my past." Evelyn looked down. "Thank you for never pressing."

Mikiko shrugged. "You're my friend. I know how private you are, and I respect that. I figure you'll tell me when you are ready."

"He was an amazing man, and we burned so hot," Evelyn said, smiling a wide grin. Mikiko had never seen Evelyn smile so big. "Not everyone saw what I saw, which always blew my mind. This was a handsome man. Smart. Loyal. Hardworking." Evelyn tugged on her necklace and started playing with the ring. "He was so funny. He could always find a way to make me laugh so hard I would tear up and double over. It was magic."

"What happened?" Mikiko asked.

Evelyn's smile faded. "Duty called. He's the type of man who was meant to do great things. I couldn't be the reason for keeping him from fulfilling his mission. So, I let him go. And that was it."

"And you haven't seen him since?" Mikiko asked, puzzled.

Evelyn smiled a sad smile.

"God, I could use a drink," Mikiko said.

Just then, Agent Cramer walked back in with a coffee. "Should I have gotten a different drink instead? Are we celebrating? Did Ori send another text?"

Evelyn quickly tucked her ring back into her blouse. "No message yet," she said.

Mikiko asked, "What did the section chief and Chivington find?"

"They said to meet them back here. They aren't here with you?" Cramer asked.

"We haven't seen either of them since they left for DC," Mikiko said.

"We've been trying to get in touch, but neither of them has been returning our calls," Evelyn added.

"They came back earlier today. All I know is that they said they would come back here to check in," Cramer replied.

"We haven't heard a single word from either of them since they left," Mikiko said.

Evelyn chimed in, "Aren't you typically attached to Appleton's hip?"

"Wait, can you track them? Did they find Ori?" Cramer asked, visibly emotional.

"Hey, what's going on?" Evelyn asked. "You seem a little on edge."

"Are you upset that you got voted off the island?" Mikiko said sarcastically.

"This is no time for joking around," Cramer snapped. "I need to know everything that you guys have on Ori and this case."

"We've told you everything," Evelyn said sternly.

"Who are you kidding, Evelyn?" Cramer shot back. This caught Evelyn off guard, as she was not used to any of her colleagues, besides Mikiko, referring to her by anything other than Agent Blackwood. "I know that you have more information that you're holding back. We are on the same team, aren't we? Trying to catch the bad guys, right?"

"I'm still not sure about that. While you may be trying to catch the 'bad guys'," Evelyn said while making air quotes with her fingers, "Agent Shikibu and I are trying to get to the truth. I'm not all that convinced that the truth and your 'bad guys' will be one and the same."

"Let's cut to it, Evelyn. What's your assessment of Ori?" Cramer asked.

"We haven't been able to find any solid evidence that Ori is guilty of anything, especially not of being the head of a large criminal organization," Evelyn said.

"I agree. I think Ori's being set up," Cramer replied.

Mikiko's jaw dropped, "Um . . . can you say that again? And I'd like to get it on the record."

"We don't have time for this. It's almost been forty-eight hours, right? And Ori is supposed to be texting you. I need everything you have on this case. I feel like I'm missing something," Cramer said with urgency.

"Why should we trust you?" Mikiko asked, narrowing her eyes.

"Because I've been allowing Evelyn to downplay her connection with Ori this entire time."

"What do you mean?" Evelyn asked.

"Let's be real, how many people can read and write straight binary code as if it's a string of emojis? Ori can, and you somehow know how to do it as well," Cramer said. "I don't believe in coincidences. Where did you learn that skill?"

"Do you think that a past connection with Ori will cloud my judgment?" Evelyn asked defiantly.

"Not at all," Cramer said. "Okay, I'm going to level with you. Deputy Director Chisolm trusts you, so I guess I trust you too. What I am about to tell you is highly confidential. This cannot leak. Do you understand?"

Both women nodded.

"I know that you are not my biggest fans. I get it. I come off like a dick, and I suck up to Appleton who, let's be real, is despicable. But that is all by design."

"What do you mean?" Evelyn asked.

"The deputy director believes that the Bureau has been and is being infiltrated by those who are secretly trying to suppress progress and democracy under the veil of patriotism. This organization is trying to maintain a type of social order that keeps a select few in power, at the expense of the majority of Americans. I'm sure you're both familiar with COINTELPRO, which was allegedly scrapped years ago, but the deputy director thinks that it's in full swing, and she thinks that Section Chief Appleton is secretly supporting the program. The deputy director also believes that Ori is the biggest threat to COINTELPRO's agenda, and in taking him down, a lot of senior members will have their fingerprints all over this. My mission is to stay as close as I can to Appleton and to identify as many members of this program as possible."

"How confident are you that this is true?" Evelyn asked.

"Very confident. There's a clear pattern across the major cases that Appleton has touched, with odd evidence and claims that the alleged criminals were set up. But the people behind COINTELPRO have deep pockets and serious political pull, which is why we are trying to identify as many senior people as possible so that we can determine their weaknesses."

"This is crazy," Mikiko said, clearly still in disbelief.

"Evelyn, the deputy director made sure that you were on this case because she knew that you would be unbiased and that you wouldn't allow anything bad to happen to Ori without knowing the entire truth. If we can't figure out where Appleton is, then Ori could be in danger."

"I believe him," Evelyn said, looking Mikiko in the eyes. She then shifted her gaze back to Special Agent Cramer. "What do you need from us?"

Chapter 34

"Do you have any idea where Ori went when he was in DC? Who was he meeting with?" Cramer asked.

Evelyn looked over to Mikiko. "Go ahead and tell him, Mikiko."

Mikiko settled in to get to work in front of her computer. "For starters, I tapped into the footage when the plane landed. I have images of everyone who got off the plane. There was only one passenger who got off the plane, and it wasn't Ori. Here's the address that this individual went to. It's the home of—"

Before Mikiko could finish, Agent Cramer said, "Silas Stillman."

"Do you know him?" Evelyn asked, eyebrows arched.

"We believe that he's—"

At that moment, they heard Ori's cell phone buzz. They got quiet as they all huddled around the phone.

"What does it say?" Mikiko asked.

"I'm not entirely sure. This one is a bit different," Evelyn said. "Let's put it into the translator just to be certain."

Evelyn rattled off the strings of ones and zeroes while Mikiko typed. Once finished, Mikiko said, "A set of coordinates?"

"Pull it up on the map," Cramer said.

"On it; here it is," Mikiko said. "Looks like the middle of the forest north of the city."

"Is there more to the message?" Cramer asked.

Evelyn was staring at the map on the large monitor. Without looking down at the phone she said, "Meet me here in exactly twenty-four hours."

"That's it?" Mikiko said. "After all of this waiting?"

"He does end the message by saying, 'Be careful'," Evelyn offered.

"That's an odd way to end the message," Cramer said.

"Not if you are a nice guy," Mikiko said.

"Let's get a move on and get to that location," Cramer said.

"Let's wait until the morning," Evelyn said, slowing him down. "We haven't had a good night's rest in a while. We know exactly where he will be and when. Let's all get a few hours of sleep so that we can be sharp. Plus, we need to figure out where Appleton and Chivington are."

"Do you think there's any chance they've figured you out?" Mikiko asked Cramer.

"Not possible. You two and the deputy director are literally the only people who know my true mission."

Cramer continued, "I just think that Appleton wanted to keep what he is up to as tight as possible."

"Tomorrow is going to be an eventful day," Mikiko said with apprehension.

"Yes, it is," Evelyn agreed. "So let's get some sleep. We will get up early and put a surveillance team in place so that we can be prepared. Mikiko, before you go, it would be a good idea to make sure that you have everything squared away here. If tomorrow goes down like I think it will, this place will be swarming with all types of people. Be sure to catalog and copy all of our evidence."

"Good call. I'll take care of it," Mikiko said.

"How long do you think it will take you to finish?" Evelyn asked.

"A couple more hours. I've already cataloged and copied almost everything. There are just a few more pieces of evidence I need to go through," Mikiko replied.

"Okay," Evelyn said. "I'm going back to my hotel. Try to wrap up quickly and get some sleep. Let's meet back here at 0600."

"I'm going to crash here; I need to make sure that I've finished . . ." Mikiko looked over at Special Agent Cramer, "cleaning up all of my files."

"Okay, see you first thing," Evelyn said as she departed.

Shortly after Evelyn left, Mikiko placed the mobile phone back in the plastic evidence bag and set it back in the evidence box.

Mikiko spent the next couple of hours cleaning up her computer hard drive, filing different pieces of evidence away. She realized that she has all of the binary messages from Ori's cell phone translated, categorized, and stored in her files, except for the last one. Mikiko went to the box containing the various pieces of evidence and removed the plastic bag with the phone.

The last message that Ori sent looked longer than Mikiko remembered from Evelyn's translation. Mikiko plugged it into the translator. "Shit!" Mikiko called out to Special Agent Cramer, who was passed out on a couple of chairs nearby. "Wake up! Evelyn lied to us. I think she's in trouble."

"What do you mean?" Cramer said, jolting upright.

"After the coordinates, the message said, 'Meet here tomorrow at 0435 if you want to see the truth. Be careful. These are dangerous times.'"

"Why would she lie?" Cramer asked.

"I'm not sure; this is not like her," Mikiko said worriedly.

"Do you think we can get there in time?" Cramer asked.

"We'll be cutting it close, but we have to try. Let's call for backup on the way," Mikiko said.

Chapter 35

Leslie opened her eyes and found herself in the front seat of a car. It was hard to get her bearings after returning to Atlanta from the island. The vehicle began to slow down as Ori and Leslie pulled up to large iron gates that were surrounded by a brick wall that stood at least six feet tall. Next to the entrance was a small red-brick guard station. As the pair approached the guard's booth, an older gentleman poked his head out. He clearly recognized Ori and said "Hey! I didn't expect to see you today. How's everything going?"

Leslie looked at him, puzzled, wondering if he'd just not been watching the news. Ori responded breezily with a broad smile, "I'm still breathing, so I can't complain."

"You said that right," the man said with a good-natured laugh.

"Sorry I'm coming by unannounced, but—"

The guard cut Ori off, "No worries, you go right on in. I'll call and give the boss a heads up to let him know you are on your way." Then the gate started to slowly open up.

Inside the gate, Leslie's eyes were immediately drawn to the large, red-brick mansion with big, white columns in front. The house had a wide front porch with a couple of charming white rocking chairs that seemed a bit out of place.

By the time Ori and Leslie were halfway down the long gravel driveway, they saw the front door open and two people come out. It was Senator Lane Whitman and his wife, Sally.

"Oh, my goodness," Sally said. She hugged Ori as soon as he got out of the car. "Are y'all alright?" she asked, her voice and face filled with concern. Her Savannah accent was sweet and prominent. Sally could make anyone lower his guard.

"Ori, I'm glad y'all are here, but I wish you would have let me know you were on your way. I would have gotten more security," the senator said as he shook Ori's hand.

"We have been worried sick about you," Sally went on. "And who is this?"

"Thank you both. This is Leslie, one of my colleagues who got caught up in this whole ordeal."

"I'm Lane, and this is my wife Sally," the senator said as he and his wife reached out to shake Leslie's hand.

"Welcome," Sally said warmly. "Let's get you both inside."

"I need a favor," Ori said to Lane. "Can we talk someplace private?"

"Of course," Lane said as he led the way to his study.

"Oh, Lane," Sally called out just before they shut the door. "May I speak with you for a minute?"

"In a moment, Sally."

"But it's important, and it will only be one minute." She put on her best smile.

Sally tried to keep her voice down as they talked in the next room, but Leslie and Ori could overhear the words *innocent, perception,* and *reputation.* There was a moment of silence just before Lane and Sally reappeared.

As they both came back around the corner, Ori said, "I need you both to know something. I'm innocent, and I plan on turning myself in for protective custody. Leslie is my head attorney, and I've signed over the entire corporation to her. I need your help to look after her and to provide some coverage and some guidance. I was also hoping some of your security could get me to the safe house." Ori looked at Sally and smiled gently. "I know how long and how hard you have been working on getting this man in the White House. I'm sure that you have sacrificed more than we could imagine, and I would never do anything to jeopardize that."

"Oh, Ori," Sally said with worry in her voice. "You just take care of yourself, okay?"

Ori nodded and the senator escorted Ori and Leslie into the living room. "Give me a few minutes to call extra security here." The senator left the room for a few minutes, and when he came back, he slipped a mobile phone into his pocket.

"Should we grab a drink? The team will be here in about ten minutes."

"Why not?" Ori replied and then asked, "Will you excuse me, I'm going to use the restroom."

"A drink for you as well, Leslie?" The senator asked as he stood in front of the bar cart, starting to pour bourbon into tumblers.

"No, I'm okay," she responded.

He then came over with his drink and had a seat across from her. "You know, Leslie, my family got started in the lending business. That's part of how we accumulated our wealth. I don't do much with it now. I've let my brother run the business while I pursue politics, but I'm sure that he will be more than happy to help you out."

"Thank you, that's very generous," Leslie said, forcing a smile. She knew this already, of course, and actually knew that the senator's brother has seen most of his success in predatory lending.

"Our family business started something like Ori's business did. We were looking out for the little guy. We used to provide loans and housing to those who couldn't afford it." The senator took a sip of his bourbon and exhaled as if he didn't have a care in the world.

Ori came back into the room, picked up his glass from the cart and took a sip. "Lane, are you giving her your origin story?"

The senator started to laugh, and then Sally walked into the room holding a phone out toward her husband. "It's your security detail."

"Thank you." He held the phone up to his ear. "Yes, yep, alright." He hung up and put the phone in his other jacket pocket. "The security team is ready; let's head out."

"Are you coming with us?" Leslie asked.

"You're staying here," Ori said. "You are at the house of a United States senator; nothing will happen to you here."

Sally nodded. "This is one of the safest places for you right now."

"Once I turn myself in, this should all be over, and you will be safe," Ori added.

"I'm going with you, Ori," the senator said.

"Lane!" Sally exclaimed with genuine surprise.

"No one would be foolish enough to attack him while he's with a sitting US senator. To hell with perception; this is my friend, and I want to make sure that he's safe. Then we will let the court system sort all of this out."

"Thank you, Lane; I appreciate it," Ori said.

"It's my pleasure."

"Ori, please, no unnecessary risks," Sally pleaded.

"I promise," Ori replied. He paused and briefly opened his mouth as if he was going to say something else, but instead, he gave Sally a polite nod and walked out with Lane right behind him.

Chapter 36

Lane settled into the back seat of the SUV next to Ori. They both gazed out the window, and the car filled with silence. The only noise was the muffled sound of the engine. Breaking the silence, Ori said, "Sometimes, I like to just think about how far we've come as a civilization."

"What do you mean?" asked Lane.

"I mean, only a hundred and fifty years ago, people were still relying on horses as a primary means of transportation. And now, we are traveling in vehicles that play music and blow cool air in the dead of summer and that are made from minerals from the earth. With the average life expectancy being eighty years old, that's only two generations ago."

Lane smiled and looked at Ori. "That is something, isn't it?"

"Do you ever wonder what the world will be like two generations after us?" Ori asked.

"Well, I'm sure that they'll be just fine. Hell, the future generations will probably be much better off than we are.

We're making the decisions necessary for my great-grandchildren to have an easy life."

Ori turned and stared at Lane. There was no smile on Ori's face, which caught Lane off guard. Lane realized that he had never seen Ori upset. Ori could always find the bright side of things. That's what he liked about Ori because it was real and refreshing. Lane was used to operating in a world full of cynics who only invested time in you if they thought that they would get some return out of it. And the most successful people were the ones who mastered the art of making everyone they interacted with feel as though they cared about them. Lane was from a world where no one could truly relate to the common man, but they could still make even a coal miner feel understood. To do this, one had to learn to put on a sincere-looking smile all the time. Lane was one of the best at this. The only face that Lane saw without a smile was his wife's, behind closed doors. He'd seen her frown for so many years, it almost didn't register with him anymore.

Ori's expression wasn't a look of sadness. It was worse than that. It was an expression of remorse. Ori looked away, probably sensing that Lane was assessing him.

"Hey," Lane said. "Everything's going to be just fine."

"Oh, I know it is," Ori replied. "I'm just going to miss this, all of this."

"What do you mean? Don't start talking all crazy on me. You are going to get through this."

Ori smiled and inhaled a long, deep breath. Then something shifted in the atmosphere of the car. Ori's chest puffed up as he continued to breathe in, and the expansion of his chest didn't stop. It's as though Ori's body mass was doubling before Lane's eyes. Lane blinked a couple of times, wondering if he was having some sort of episode, but the picture in front of him did not normalize. Ori held his breath for a few seconds, and then as he exhaled, what looked like a million tiny, shiny particles floated from Ori's mouth. It was mesmerizing and almost beautiful. As Lane watched, some particles rose toward the roof of the car. As soon as the particles made contact with the fabric, the entire roof of the car erupted in flames. Lane screamed, despite himself, and panicked. He looked frantically toward his guys in the front, but they somehow seemed oblivious to what was happening. So he yelled out, "Hey, hey . . , What the hell is going on? Are you guys going to do something?" The guards continued looking forward at the dark road as if all was well. Lane was sweating and having trouble breathing. "Guys, the car is on fire!" he yelled one last attempt. "Pull over now!"

He could see very little through the smoke and particles. Then he heard the calm voice of Ori. "Don't waste your breath. They can't hear you. Do you think that I don't know what you are planning? Do you think that I'm that ignorant? Why would you agree to something like this?"

Lane stammered, "W— What are you talking a—"

"Please, do not insult me by lying," Ori cut him off. Lane could see his outline looming large, and his voice sounded as though it could be coming out of the speakers in the car. "I'm well aware of what you've been up to. Is it worth it?"

"I— I don't know," Lane said softly, looking around, searching for an answer as the flames surrounded them. "Please!" Lane pleaded.

"How can I make this stop? You brought this here. Only you can make it right," Ori said.

"How?" Lane found himself shouting. The flames were crawling up his clothes, and he tried to beat them down.

"It's simple; do the right thing. But to do that, you will have to decide if it's worth it. Is it worth it?" The air between them somehow cleared just enough to see Ori more plainly. He was facing Lane, but he was different. His skin was as black as night. He no longer had any physical features. Ori had the shape of a man but without the defining characteristics of one. Where his skin used to be, now all Lane could see was a billion tiny star-like lights, each no bigger than a period.

"What is happening?" Lane whispered, seeing that the drivers were still focused on the road as if nothing was happening. "Who are you?"

"That isn't the question you should be asking right now. The question you should be asking is, who are *you*, and is it worth it?"

Lane closed his eyes as tightly as he could as he felt the flames engulf his body and make their way to his chest. As soon as the fire reached his chest, the flames converted to a crude oil–like substance. It was cold, black, and shiny. It oozed around his body, extending down to his toes and wrapping around him up to his shoulders. The black matter then began to tighten, suffocating him.

"I— I can't breathe," Lane said weakly, beginning to cry, as the blanket of darkness continued to tighten around him.

"Is. It. Worth. It?" Ori's presence asked, still facing Lane. Then a woman's voice screamed loudly, "Is it?" The shriek shattered all the windows in the SUV. Lane squeezed his eyes shut.

"Sir?"

Lane jumped.

"Are you okay?" the guard in the passenger seat continued, staring at the senator.

Lane looked around the car to see Ori sitting next to him, looking normal and at ease. Lane looked around the interior of the car to see that everything was still intact. There were no signs of a fire. Lane quickly looked down at his body and touched his chest and legs, realizing that he was free to move around.

The guard continued, "I think you may have fallen asleep, sir, and had a bad dream."

Ori's face was turned slightly away from the Senator toward the window. He appeared blissfully relaxed as if his worries were behind him. The car then got quiet again, and Lane's breathing slowed to normal. "Just a dream. It was just a dream," he reassured himself.

Then Lane's cellphone buzzed, breaking the silence in the car. He looked down and then told his fellow passengers, "I'm sorry. I've got to take this."

Lane turned to look out of the window and listened to the voice on the other end of the phone. Choosing his words thoughtfully, he said, "Yes, we are together. I'm taking full responsibility for him. We don't know who to trust, so I want us to personally oversee his delivery to the protective detail that the president allowed us to get for him."

Lane turned to Ori and smiled. Lane continued talking, turning back to face the window. "Once you arrive at the location I sent, have your men debrief and relieve the two guards. I don't want them to spend too much time up here. We don't need anybody getting tired on the job," the senator said as he looked toward his men in the front of the car.

The driver and the security guard in the passenger seat looked at each other and then faced straight ahead again.

"We will wait for you inside." Lane continued, "Ori is critical to me, so we need to get this right. Only bring people you trust. We can't have Ori be at any risk."

The men rode in silence for the next hour.

Chapter 37

"De qué estas hablando?" Jackeline said, laughing, with a smile on her face.

Nicolas knew that he should never have allowed himself to fall for her, but he did. He loved the way the strands of her dirty-blonde hair would cover part of her beautiful face when she put her head down to laugh.

"What are you talking about?" she repeated in English, nudging him playfully. They were sitting on one of his favorite benches in Piedmont Park. "What do you mean you always come here? You've never once told me about this place," Jackeline said.

Nicolas loved to sit under the gazebo and feed the turtles and the ducks that call the pond in the middle of the park their home. "Te lo he dicho un millón de veces," Nicolas said, smiling and nudging Jackeline back.

"You've told me a million times? Really?" she said with a sarcastic smile. "Oh, the many secretos de Nicolas."

It was a sunny but chilly day in the park. Nicolas felt so ecstatic to be there with Jackeline, and he couldn't understand why. He watched her lean over the edge of the gazebo wall and gently toss chunks of a baguette into the water. Her expression was so carefree and so full of joy that it made Nicolas feel warm inside. Jackeline was wearing a sleeveless red and navy sundress, and when the breeze blew, it perfectly framed her silhouette.

He didn't realize he was smiling until Jackeline turned around and said, "What? Te estás burlando de mí? Are you laughing at me?"

"No, no." He laughed. "I would never make fun of you. I was just admiring the view."

"Oh yeah?" Jackeline asked. With a devilish smile, she slowly walked toward Nicolas. Both of her hands were clutching the bottom of her dress, and with every slow step she took toward him, she pulled her dress up an inch.

Nicolas smiled, thinking about how perfect a day this could end up being, but then he realized that something was slightly off. It's a beautiful weekend day, and we are the only two people in the park? What's going on?

Nicolas turned around, surveying the surrounding areas, looking for at least one other soul in the park. As he focused his gaze in the distance, he felt Jackeline's body plop down on the bench next to him. Startled by the uncharacteristic lack of grace, he turned to look at her. She was leaning in close to his face and staring intensely back at him. Nicolas pulled his head back to get a better look at her face, and he realized that something had changed. Her hair was no longer down and was instead in a tight ponytail as if she was going to work. Nicolas looked down and saw that her outfit had changed as well to jeans and a blazer.

"Qué está pasando?" Nicolas asked, confused. "Why are you wearing that? When did you change?"

"Nothing changed," Jackeline said. "I've been wearing this the whole time."

Nicolas heard footsteps and faint voices from behind. He turned and stared at the concrete path approaching the gazebo, waiting for someone to appear from behind the trees. As the voices got closer and louder, he had tunnel vision on the concrete path, and everything else went hazy. He sensed Jackeline trying to get his attention, but he was unable to break his gaze away from the path. Jackeline grabbed his biceps and shook him back and forth to no avail.

His sense of unease grew. "Something's wrong, why are we the only two people here? Where is everyone?" Nicolas said out loud. "Who's there?" Nicolas shouted to the footsteps and the voices that seemed to be approaching on the path but never arriving.

"Who's there? Show yourselves!" Nicolas yelled again, panicked and gaze still locked on the concrete path. "Tú no sabes quien soy? Or what I can do to you," Nicolas said, trying to mask the fear with whatever bravado he had left.

All of a sudden, the voice coming from Jackeline's seat changed to a calm, steady masculine voice, a voice that made Nicolas's heart speed up and testicles contract into his stomach. "Oh, I know exactly who you are Nicolas," the voice said.

Nicolas quickly turned around and saw Carlos sitting next to him. Carlos stood from the bench, slowly walked over to the water and tossed a few pieces of bread to the turtles.

"Lo más importante," Carlos said, "I have learned what you are capable of doing."

Once again, Nicolas heard footsteps behind him. He turned to see Jackeline, standing in her red and navy sundress again, but this time it was different. Jacki looked sad. She had lost her smile and her vibrant glow. Her hair was down on her shoulders, but it looked like she hasn't brushed it in days. Her skin was extremely pale, with a faint tinge of blue. She looked weak. She stared past Nicolas at the trees surrounding the far edge of the pond.

"Jacki," Nicolas said. "Did he hurt you? Qué pasó?" His eyes started to tear up.

"No," Jackeline said, eyes still fixated on the trees. "Papa didn't do this." Her voice was still soft and sweet. She locked eyes with Nicolas. "You did."

The sky quickly turned dark, and Nicolas glanced up. When he looked back to Jackeline, he noticed a dark circular spot on the side of her head. The spot rapidly expanded while Jackeline's eyes seemed to be fixated on the tree line, showing no reaction.

"Qué pasó mi amor? What's wrong?" Nicolas jumped up to hold her and looked more closely at the growing dark spot on her head. She didn't respond at all to his embrace. He examined the area on her head and realized that it was blood.

Nicolas panicked and shouted, "We need a doctor right away!"

"Oh, do we now?" Carlos's voice came out of nowhere. Nicolas saw him still standing by the pond, tossing in pieces of bread. "Why is that?"

"You want to save her life, don't you?"

"Why do you care all of a sudden, Nicolas? It was you who put her in this situation. You did this. You made your decision, and now there's no taking it back," Carlos said.

"No, we can fix this. I can fix this. There's still time," Nicolas said. "There's still time," he repeated to himself.

"Hey!" Carlos shouted to regain Nicolas's attention.

Nicolas started to turn away.

"Hey!" Nicolas felt hands on his shoulders as he was jerked around to face Carlos. Nicolas realized that he had never stared Carlos in the eyes before. Nicolas's heart was racing, and his body felt paralyzed. The color of Carlos's eyes transformed from dark brown to orangey-red.

Carlos smiled a wicked smile. "Now that I have your full attention, I must inform you that you are officially out of time. You are now mine."

Nicolas closed his eyes as hard as he could and used all of his strength to jerk away from Carlos's tight grip on his shoulders.

Nicolas pulled free and opened his eyes to find himself on his couch in his apartment. He closed his eyes and lets out a sigh of relief. "That was only a dream," he said to himself.

He looked around at the mess that was his apartment. He tried to lift himself off of his couch but realized that he was incredibly weak. His vision was a little hazy and his head cloudy. He finally stumbled up from his seat and turned on the lantern on the coffee table. As he shut his eyes to allow them to adjust to the light, he heard a voice in his apartment and jumped.

"Hola, Nicolas." It was a woman's voice that he had not heard before.

"Who are you, and what are you doing in my apartment?" Nicolas asked as his eyes flew open and he tried to stand up quickly, reaching for the cold metal of his gun that he kept on the coffee table.

"I moved it," the lady said. "You were on a lot of drugs, and I didn't think that it was safe to keep it close to you.

We don't want you to have any accidents." Her voice expressed concern.

Nicolas stayed quiet now, examining his visitor.

"We have a mutual connection, and they clearly can't be seen interacting in public with you. So, I was asked to check in on you if you didn't leave the apartment for more than a few days," the lady said. "I work as a nurse, so I, unfortunately, have seen my fair share of drug users." The strange lady walked into the kitchen and pulled a coffee cup out of the microwave.

Who is this mutual friend? Did Jackeline put this lady up to this? No, not possible, Nicolas thought. Then the terrible feeling of remorse he had been trying to drown came rushing back.

"Oh, god," Nicolas said to himself, but loudly enough to be heard by his visitor. "I've done something terrible." Then he looked up at her. "Thank you for checking in on me, but please, please leave me alone. I deserve what I'm doing to myself. I don't need to be saved."

"Here, drink this," the lady said as she offered Nicolas the mug.

"Gracias," he said, accepting the mug and taking a sip. "But again, I don't—"

"Shhh, please, take another drink. This tea will be good for you," the lady said with a smile.

Nicolas started to feel relaxed. "What is this?" He heard his speech starting to slur. "It's some good stuff."

The lady then looked back toward the door, as if expecting someone to come in.

"Whaass goooing onnn?" Nicolas slurred. He tried to stand up, but his limbs wouldn't cooperate. Two tall, athletic men in suits entered the living room. *Geez, ease off the steroids,* he thought to himself.

"Está listo?" one of them asked.

"Yes, he's ready," the lady responded.

"Whooo the . . ." Nicolas tried to say, but his mouth was like glue. He was still unable to stand and his breathing was becoming more burdensome.

"Ammm I dyyyying?" Nicolas asked, almost wistfully.

One of the men chuckled.

"Chill, bro," the other one said. "It's all good. You aren't going to die. Well, not today anyway. That drink will help you chill out for the trip, homie."

"You think that people who have done what you have done would go out like this?" the other man asked. "Yo, bro, that meth you were smoking must have been really special if it made you think that. Now go to sleep, we'll see you soon."

Chapter 38

Nicolas flashed in and out of consciousness as the drugs began to leave his system. When he finally came to, his eyes locked onto a beautiful nurse checking the machines that were connected to his body. "Where am I?"

The nurse slightly turned her head and gave him a puzzled look.

"Where am I? How long have I been here?" He tried to grab her arm as she started to turn away and realized that his wrists were strapped to the metal rails on the bed.

The nurse walked quickly out of the room and an older male doctor came in. "Hello, Nicolas. What seems to be the problem?" the doctor asked while picking up Nicolas's chart. Nicolas recognized the accent but couldn't place the face. The doctor was a respectable-looking man in his forties with salt-and-pepper hair and a clean-shaven face.

The doctor flipped through the pages of Nicolas's chart. "It seems like your vitals are doing just fine. You should be all nice and hydrated, but I'll make sure to get you one more IV."

Nicolas, now a bit more collected, asked again, "Where am I, and how long have I been here?"

The doctor lifted his glance slightly above the medical record folder, locking eyes with Nicolas. The doctor slowly raised his head further and smiled. "Why Nicolas, you are home, and you haven't been here nearly long enough."

Nicolas started to look around for anything familiar.

"See," the doctor continued, "the boss wanted to make sure that we do your punishment justice. We couldn't let you be so doped up that you wouldn't be able to appreciate what's in store for you. The boss wanted to make sure that you were as healthy as can be. Though those withdrawals themselves were probably torture."

As Nicolas stared down at the IVs in his arms, he heard a familiar voice filling the room. "Hola, Nicolas. Como te sientes? You know, I want to make sure that you are comfortable with this part. You see, I liked you. You had ambition and drive, all remarkable things, but you were vain, my friend. That was your downfall. Understand this: We are all born in the belly of the beast, on one end of the spectrum or the other. The choices that we make in this life steer us closer to or farther from heaven. I feel sorry for you because you had little choice in all of this. You were born here, in my pueblito. This violence, this lifestyle, is all you've ever known. So, I made a deal with an old friend. I allowed you to have something beautiful and live away from here. But you chose to destroy that beauty, to put out that light. So now, you will live the rest of your days yearning for just a touch of beauty."

When the message was over, the doctor nodded, watching Nicolas's face. "We needed you to be conscious and healthy to hear that message. Here is what is ahead of you. Your body will feel like it's in the worst possible withdrawal until you go insane. Your mind will be on a constant loop, experiencing all of the energy that you've put out into the world. Unfortunately for you, you've done more harm than good."

Chapter 39

"Jessica, can you come in here?" M's voice called out from her office.

M was editor-in-chief at the online media company, Str8 Truth Media. She was the most senior member of the company, and it was her life. Each day, she was the first in and the last out, always.

"What's up, M?" Jessica asked as she walked in.

"Great job on your last piece. 'How Long Will the New Camelot Last?' has gotten ten million views in forty-eight hours," M said.

Jessica smiled with pride. "Thanks. I guess I tapped into something a lot of people were curious about or perhaps hopeful for."

"And what do you *really* think? Has our society put our violent ways behind us?" M asked.

"Well," Jessica paused, taking a seat across from M, "I think that everything is cyclical. If we are truly living in the next age of Camelot, then at some point, I suppose it must end. I'm just not sure when that will be. I mean, most people thought that the original Camelot was a myth. Three thousand years from now, people will think that our society was a myth."

M continued her line of questioning. "Hm . . . and you propose that President Lane Whitman was a key factor leading to this time of peace?"

"If you look at the data, the violence in the US dropped significantly after he took office," Jessica said.

"His second term ended years ago," M said. "Many don't think his presidency was all that memorable."

"Maybe that's a good thing," Jessica replied. She loved a good debate. "On paper, he had an extraordinarily successful presidency—no major scandals and a very stable economy throughout his eight years. That's more than we can say for a lot of presidencies." Jessica leaned forward. "What I found most impressive is what occurred near the end of his second term and after."

"Why is that?" M asked.

"President Lane Whitman was the last male to hold that position," Jessica said. "And it was he who endorsed the candidate who became the first woman African-American president. *And*," Jessica said, on a roll, "he crossed party lines to do so—unheard of at that time."

"Any ideas on why he did that?" M asked.

"That is what I haven't figure out. I was never able to reach the former president or anyone who could speak on his behalf. But this is my train of thought. Since President

Lane Whitman's term, our society, which is globally influential, has consistently moved in a positive direction. It's been three years since an act of terrorism. Tribal conflicts around the world have quieted. The Organisation for Economic Co-operation and Development's data on reading, mathematics, and scientific knowledge are at the highest levels they've been, both within and outside the US."

M said with a smile, "Sounds a little too good to be true."

"There is a faction within the government which still has some pretty considerable influence in key areas. They believe that this period of peace is weakening our nation's grip on the world stage and putting us at risk of being conquered. But, if former war-torn countries continue finding balance and peace, then this faction should be kept in check."

M nodded and then said, "I actually called you in here because I have an assignment for you."

"An assignment? You haven't given me an assignment in years," Jessica said with surprise.

"This is a special assignment, and I need my best person on it," M said. "I need someone who isn't afraid to ask questions, and more importantly, I need someone who will listen to the answers."

"I'm officially intrigued," Jessica said. "What's the assignment?"

"What do you remember about the disappearance of Ori Clayborn?" M asked. "You were probably relatively young at the time."

"I was, but I oddly do remember it. I mean, I didn't understand what was happening, but I remember a lot of people were talking about it. Someone who was involved in his disappearance was from my hometown. In fact, he was a local hero, so the town was completely shocked to learn that he was somehow involved," Jessica said.

"I hadn't realized that you had a connection. That's going to be really helpful," M said. "That news story was all over the media until the focus shifted to the presidential election."

"That's right! That was the year that President Whitman won his first term," Jessica said, the memories clicking into place.

"Yep," M nodded. "Ori Clayborn disappeared right before Lane Whitman began his campaign and Ori's story got lost in the noise—until now. An anonymous person reached out to me, offering to pay an absurd amount of money to find out what happened to him."

"Wonder why they chose us. And how much is an absurd amount?"

"If you can do what you are great at, then they are willing to fund this company's costs for the next ten years." M looked out her office window to the staff working at their desks. "And if they allow us to publish it, then—"

Jessica cut her off. "What do you mean *if* they allow us to publish it?"

"That's the stipulation. They want to read the article first and then decide if they will allow us to publish it. If the anonymous funder allows us to publish the article, then the story will be exclusively ours," M said with a wide grin on her face. "So, you in?"

"I'm in," Jessica replied.

"Perfect." M placed her hand on an envelope on her desk and slid it across to Jessica. "Here's an airline ticket to Phoenix. There will be a rental car waiting for you as well as a hotel reservation in your hometown." Jessica looked at M skeptically.

M began typing at her computer as if she was alone in her office. "What are you still doing here? I've got work to do. Go! Your flight leaves in a matter of hours, and I'm sure you have some packing to do."

As Jessica turned to leave M's office, M added, "One more thing, take that manila envelope on my bookshelf on your way out. It contains background information to get you up to speed on your research." The buff-colored folder was at least a couple of inches thick.

A few hours later, as Jessica settled into her window seat on the airplane, she pulled out the large, thick envelope. As she started to open it, she wondered how M knew she would say yes. Jessica put her tray table down and emptied the contents of the folder. It held pictures and profiles of people who had been interviewed during the investigation. There were also pages and pages of documents with at least half of the words blacked out. "Why even give me something with half of the information redacted?" Jessica whispered to herself. The other object in the manila file folder was a business card, or at least something the size of a standard business card. But this one had no company name or logo on it. There wasn't even the name of an individual, merely a phone number.

Jessica thought about her assignment and let out a long sigh. *So, I need to find out what happened to Silas to then find out what happened to Ori,* she thought to herself.

She started letting her mind wander back to when this all happened. After the news broke in their town that Silas was the primary suspect in the disappearance of a successful businessman, everyone in the town started gossiping. Silas had disappeared too, but the assumption was that he had gone into hiding. Word around town was that he would always find a way to let his parents know that he was alive. It was the Silas case that made Jessica want to get into journalism. She and Silas both attended the same high school, several years apart, but she remembered that his name was plastered all over the place. He was king of the school while there and then found a way out of the small town too. He became a world-traveling hero. She remembered thinking that there had to be a complicated story that just wasn't being told.

A little turbulence brought Jessica's mind back to the present. She was never a fan of flying and only tolerated it when it was necessary. If it were up to her, she would drive everywhere. Jessica neatly placed the documents back inside the envelope, tucked it into her bag, and raised her seatback tray. As the air smoothed out, she allowed her head to lay against the headrest. Jessica closed her eyes and nodded off.

Chapter 40

Jessica figured that the best place to start her investigation was at Silas's parents' house. Since Jessica's parents had moved to Florida after her graduation from high school, this was the first time Jessica had been back to her hometown since she left for college. It was odd being here. Even though she grew up here, it had never really felt like home. Jessica realized early on that she didn't really fit in here. She had always been the artistic type. She loved getting lost in a good book, going to see a show at the closest theater, and spending hours either painting or writing in her journal.

She had always thought that this was the perfect town for someone like Silas. It was a typical military town, relatively small, primarily existing because of the adjacent army base, a training site for elite intelligence soldiers. The town was surrounded by beautiful mountains and shared a border with Mexico. In high school, she had heard rumors of a dark underbelly of her hometown but never really put much stock in these stories. It was a pretty pleasant place to live if you were into outdoor activities, sports, and spending time with family. People like Silas thrived in this environment.

As she pulled into the neighborhood where Silas grew up, she noticed that every home she passed had the American flag proudly flying. She remembered that her parents always made it a point to show support for the troops in this way. She was touched by this collective display of patriotism that was clearly a part of everyday life, not just reserved for holidays. Jessica had called ahead, and as she parked in front of Silas's parents' house, they both came outside and waved at her.

"Hello," Jessica said as she got out of the car. "I'm Jessica. It's so nice to meet you both."

"Welcome," Mr. Stillman said.

"Oh, thank you so much for coming," Mrs. Stillman said warmly. The pair invited Jessica into the house.

"Thank you for having me, Mr. and Mrs. Stillman," Jessica said.

"It's Maureen and Frank. No need to be so formal," Frank said while walking her into the house. Jessica entered their living room to find a full spread of food on the coffee table.

Maureen and Frank were surprisingly youthful for folks in their late sixties. They explained how Silas was the product of a teenage romance that everyone thought would eventually flame out. After Maureen became pregnant, Frank moved in with Maureen and her family. The couple had been together ever since.

Maureen noticed Jessica staring at the food. "I probably got a little carried away—Frank told me I was—but we are just so excited that you are going to find out what happened to our boy."

"Oh, Mrs. Stillman, thank you. I actually haven't eaten much, so this is perfect," Jessica lied, but she realized that the longer she stayed, the more at ease she'll put Mr. and Mrs. Stillman.

"Did you say on the phone that you are from here? Did you go to school with our Silas?" Frank asked.

"Look at her, Franky," Maureen teased. "She's such a vibrant young thing. Way too young to have gone to school with Silas."

Jessica smiled. "I was a few years younger than Silas, but I actually grew up in this same neighborhood. My house was just a few streets from here."

"Oh, wow! Are you staying with your parents while you are in town?" Maureen asked.

"Oh, no, I have a room at the hotel in town," Jessica replied.

Maureen asked, slightly exasperated, "Is this a generational thing? Why don't you want to stay with your parents when you come back home?"

"Sorry." Jessica realized that she hit a sensitive topic. "I totally would stay with my parents if they were here, but they moved to Florida after I graduated from high school. That's where my parents are from originally."

Sensing that Maureen was comforted with this answer, Jessica asked, "Did Silas come into town and not stay with you?"

Chapter 41

Jessica pulled out her recorder. "Is it okay if I record this so that I can have it on record?"

"Of course, that's no problem," both Maureen and Frank said.

"Great." Jessica pressed the record button on her device. "What can you tell me about your son Silas?"

Frank heaved a big sigh, "I guess I can start from the beginning. You see, when Maureen and I were expecting Silas, my family and community did not approve, and I was excommunicated. That meant that I was cut off from my family, friends, and any support. Maureen didn't come from much, but her family took me in with open arms."

"It was a house full of love, but we didn't have much of anything else, and we really had some hard financial times. Silas always wanted more, and he felt like he had something to prove," Maureen added.

Frank interjected, "I think that he believed that it was his fault that we had some financial issues."

"Frank's side of the family was wealthy. Some think that one of the reasons we were cut off was a perception that I was a poor girl trying to trap him with a baby," Maureen said.

"Over time, I started my own business. It was enough to keep a roof over our heads, put food on the table, and clothes on our backs," Frank said proudly.

"But again, Silas dreamed of more," Maureen told Jessica.

"Silas always believed that the military was the path to a great future. He used to read all of these history books and told me that if you don't have money, then one of the only honest ways to significantly move up in social status is by becoming a high-ranking officer in the military," Frank said.

"He was so determined, our boy," Maureen said. "He saw Frank struggle to keep the family business afloat."

"I couldn't compete with big-box stores and their lower-priced goods. It was a losing fight and ultimately wasn't enough to make ends meet," Frank said.

Maureen took a drink from the mug she held. "We think that really impacted Silas. *Family Owned* and *Made in America* weren't enough to keep people from going to the outskirts of town and buying cheap imports. 'Fucking NAFTA,' Silas used to say."

"Pardon her French," Frank said, and Maureen swiped at him playfully.

Maureen continued, "I think that the final straw for Silas was watching Frank go from owning his own store and being his own boss to working in a cubicle for someone else." Maureen sighed. "That business was our livelihood, and when we lost it, Frank needed a job. His manager was such an incompetent jerk. But . . ." Maureen paused. "His uncle was someone important, which meant that Frank's boss thought that he was important too."

"It was the best job I could find," Frank said. "No one wanted to hire a failed business owner. That job slowly broke me down."

"Silas felt that an honest man doesn't get far in the corporate world. He was convinced that the only people who were extremely successful must have done something crooked to get that success," Maureen said.

"When he was in school, all that mattered to him was maintaining academic eligibility to play ball and wrestle. That and history class. Nothing much else mattered," Frank said with a shake of the head.

"That's right." Maureen's face lit up with a smile. "He loved his history, especially American history."

"That boy would read any and everything that talked about the blood, sweat, and tears that went into making our country the greatest in the world. He strongly believed in our democracy." Frank continued, "My son knew exactly what he was getting involved with when he joined the service. Well, at least early on. All he ever wanted to do was serve his country as best he could. He was proud of that work. He would do it all again if he could."

"Well, at least we think that he would. After several combat tours, well, you know, he started to change. He began to question what it was that he was doing. Questioning if he was a true patriot," Maureen said.

"What do you mean, questioning if he was a true patriot?" Jessica asked.

"He made one passing comment, Maureen," Frank blurted out.

"But still, when has our Silas ever made a comment questioning his patriotism?" Maureen fired back.

As Frank searched for an answer, Maureen continued, "You should speak to Michelle, if you haven't already."

"Michelle?" Jessica asked.

"Michelle Lukwago," Maureen said. Then she and Jessica said in unison, "Christian Lukwago's little sister."

Jessica remembered reading Christian Lukwago's obituary years ago. She hadn't thought about him or his sister in years. Jessica remembered reading a piece in their local newspaper about the Lukwago kids. Both were talented student-athletes, and Christian received a scholarship to the Naval Academy. Christian and Michelle's father was originally from Mississippi. He enlisted in the army after high school, and while on deployment, he met their mom, who was originally from Uganda. Even though this town had families stationed here from all over the US, the Lukwagos were the only family who had African roots. Christian's name was also plastered all over Jessica's high school, usually next to Silas's. They were a phenomenal team. People said Christian was even more talented than Silas.

"How does Michelle fit into this?" Jessica asked.

"Silas, Christian, and Michelle were all really close," Maureen said.

"Does Michelle still live in town?" Jessica asked.

"Yeah, she moved back home to live with her parents after Christian died," Frank said.

"Moved back? Where was she before?" Jessica asked.

"She was back east with the boys. They all had a house together," Maureen said. "Michelle doesn't like to talk much about Silas and her brother, but if anyone knows anything, it will be Michelle."

"Thank you for all of the information. I know this must be hard to talk about," Jessica acknowledged.

"No, thank you for your interest. No one has ever come to try and figure out what happened to our boy. I had faith that you would come," Maureen said as she gave Jessica a long, comforting hug. "Our Silas was a little rough around the edges, and yes, I'm sure he's done some things that he regrets, but our Silas would never knowingly harm an innocent person. You'll see."

Chapter 42

Jessica approached Michelle's house and was shocked to see how unkempt the yard was. Weeds two feet tall were growing in between the white decorative rocks that filled the front yard. Judging by the small, brick structure, it appeared that there was once a garden in the front yard, but it's now overrun with more weeds.

The front door opened as Jessica got closer. Michelle Lukwago was standing there in long, black spandex pants and a pink tank top, with sweat seeping down around her neck and collarbone. Michelle looked like she could win the state track and field championships again tomorrow.

"Come on in," Michelle said. "Sorry if I smell. I just got back from a long run."

"No worries. Thank you for taking the time to see me," Jessica said.

"No problem at all. It's not like I'm super busy," Michelle said before taking a swig from her large, sports water bottle. "This is a pretty big deal if DC's top investigative reporter is here in my parents' house to meet with me."

Caught a little off guard, Jessica asked, "You've read my work?"

"It's not every day that a kid from your hometown moves to DC and makes big waves," Michelle said before she took another drink from the bottle.

"I didn't think anyone from here would have a taste for my type of journalism," Jessica said.

"Well, you do tend to tell the truth. Sometimes, people would rather feel comfortable." Michelle continued, "Ignorance is bliss and all that."

Jessica nodded her head ever so slightly as she considered this remark.

"Maureen called and said you were coming over. You are looking into what happened to Silas, right?" Michelle asked.

"Yeah, it's not common for the head security member of one of the country's top politicians to vanish without a trace, and no one looks into it," Jessica said. "What do you know about Silas and the line of work he was in?"

"Silas is extremely resourceful. If he wants to hide and not be found, he can totally do that. He's hiding in shame," Michelle spat the words out angrily.

"Shame for . . .?" Jessica waited for Michelle to fill the blank.

"He sold his soul," Michelle said, barely above a whisper.

"What do you mean?" Jessica asked.

Michelle looked Jessica in the eye and seemed to be deciding something. Then after a moment, she asked, "What do you know about me, my brother, and Silas?"

Jessica shrugged. "Not much, to be honest. Because of the nature of your brother and Silas's missions. And we both know the military won't let me anywhere near their records. All I've been able to piece together so far is that you used to live with them for a while. Then, after your brother's death, Silas took a job working for some political consulting group. I think that a former US senator founded it. You moved back home, and Silas kept working for the politician for years. Then, suddenly, he went missing, was blamed for a prominent disappearance, and no one on Capitol Hill even batted an eye."

"Silas didn't take a job working for the politician after my brother's death. That assignment, or *path*," Michelle said mockingly, "was offered to him well before my brother was killed. They had been trying to get Silas for a while."

"Who's they?" Jessica asked, thinking that she was starting to get somewhere.

"I'm not sure. Silas and Christian would always say *they*. Silas was tapped as someone with high potential. They appreciated his valor and dedication and talked about the remarkable things he could do for our country. They never told him what exactly he would be doing. That information was revealed only after he accepted the job. The one perk was that he would no longer have to go on these suicide missions. Or at least I thought that was a perk. Silas was stubborn. He and my brother had been on so many assignments together. They were an effective team. Silas didn't trust his safety with anyone else. Chris finally convinced him to take the job. That way, at least one of them would be around to look after me." Michelle laughed as a tear rolled down her cheek. She took a deep breath and visibly tried to shake the sadness away. "Ironic, isn't it?"

"What's ironic about it?" Jessica asked.

"Once Silas took the job, he and I were over," Michelle said.

"I'm confused, what do you mean, over?" Jessica asked, feeling like she missed something.

"Silas and I were engaged. He proposed after he accepted the job. Silas figured that since he wouldn't be sent on crazy missions anymore, then we could finally settle down and start a family. What he didn't account for was that his new role wouldn't permit such a relationship," Michelle said with her arms crossed and her nostrils flaring. "After he worked for a while, he realized that I was still a liability, so he called off the engagement. When I pressed him about it, he told me that having feelings for me would prevent him from carrying out his duty to his country."

"I'm so sorry," Jessica said.

"We weren't very public with our relationship, so at least I didn't have to come back home embarrassed," Michelle said as she forced a smile.

"When did this happen?" Jessica asked.

"That was about a year or so after he took that job," Michelle answered. "He moved out of the apartment the next day, and I didn't see or hear from him for a year. I was out with some friends and saw him being pretty cozy with some woman at the bar."

"Did you say anything to him?" Jessica asked.

"Of course, I did. The look on Silas's face when I approached him was classic. He was so shocked. It's a rare thing when Silas Stillman is short for words." Michelle smiled ruefully.

"Did you guys ever talk after that?" Jessica asked.

"He tried to call me a couple of times, but I never felt like speaking to him. After my brother found out about my little encounter with him at the bar, Chris told me that he would talk to Silas about it. After Chris called Silas out for it, they stopped speaking as well. That had to hurt; they were best friends," Michelle said. "Then a few months later, Chris was killed on a mission."

"When was the last time you heard from Silas?" Jessica asked.

"I received a letter from him a few years ago," Michelle said. She walked over to the kitchen island and pulled a folded envelope out of a drawer. Michelle handed the unopened envelope over to Jessica.

Jessica noticed the slightly tan color of the document, a result of its age. "You've never opened it?" she asked.

"I've thought about it, I really have, but I don't think that there's anything in there that would make things right. At the end of the day, he made his decision, and his choice wasn't me or Chris. I'm sure that Silas was able to justify his choice, and that's good for him. Knowing Silas the way that I do, that letter was his way of making peace with his own actions, not with me. If he wanted to make peace with me, then it would be him I'd be holding, not this envelope," Michelle said, looking down at her hands. "I don't know why I kept it, but I'm glad I did. When his parents told me that he went missing again, I wasn't too concerned because, in his line of work, that comes with the territory: do what's necessary to serve and protect our country. But since you are here, looking into Silas, I figure why not give this to you. Maybe something good will come out of it."

Chapter 43

Michelle let Jessica use the little office on the first floor. Jessica used her fingers to trace the edge of the envelope. She felt the hard outline of a small, square object, about the size of her fingernail. When Jessica opened the envelope, she found a red cube that looked like a rubber keychain. Inside the keychain was a thin, black piece of plastic. It was an SD card, accompanied by a handwritten letter.

Jessica started with the letter, which read:

Michelle,

I know I let you and Christian down; I'm sorry about that. I was so focused on giving everything to protect what I believed in that I forgot what I was doing it for. Everything I've done is because I believe in love and happiness and freedom. I was proud to sacrifice whatever it took so that every hardworking American could enjoy what I believe in. I was proud to defend my beliefs, but I've crossed a line. What goes around always comes around, and I know that soon, I'll pay for what I've done. I've tried to do the best I can to set things right, but only God knows if I've done enough.

Yours,

Silas

Jessica then searched through the different files on the SD card. She noticed a file that had a particularly large file size. Upon opening it, she saw that it was a four-hundred-page document, which on its own didn't justify its large file size. Jessica scanned the document and found a small icon for a video file halfway through. She double-clicked on the icon, and the video media player became a full-screen display with a familiar face. Jessica clicked her mouse cursor over the play button, and Silas began to speak.

"Love, I want to start by telling you I'm so sorry for walking away from us. I did so with the best of intentions. Please believe me when I say that I wanted to do my best to serve our country and protect the beautiful life that I want you to have.

"If you are watching this video, something unfortunate has happened to me. I don't expect this video to save me because I knew the risks when I signed up for the job. I'm creating this video because, at some point, the role that was meant to protect the freedoms for which so many have sacrificed has morphed into something else. Something worse.

"My job was to do what was necessary to protect our nation. At times, that required me to do things that most people couldn't stomach. I understand that freedom doesn't come free. Things must be done, things that no man should have to do. To protect the nation that I love, I took my job very seriously. I've seen the work of the monsters out there who threaten our democracy and the freedom that we Americans enjoy. When I was offered the role, I knew that to stop these monsters, I'd have to become a monster myself. We started out focusing on the traditional places: terrorists in the Middle East, North Korea, and Russia. Then the threats started moving closer, to cartels collaborating to smuggle terrorists into the United States and to extremists who were American citizens trying to infiltrate the highest level of government."

Silas looked down. "The lines were officially blurred. We were going after targets that didn't look like targets, but we were assured they were a threat." Silas lifted his head, and he looked tired. "Finally, it struck me. I had been fighting—no, we had been fighting this entire time because we've been told that was the only way to bring the change needed to achieve peace. But what I realized is that peace and change were not the end goal for those who were handing me the orders. Chaos, calamity, and constant fear kept them in business."

Silas laughed like he had been foolish. He slowly rubbed his face and beard. "I shouldn't have been surprised by that. Any student of history knows that the most studied great civilizations used the military and war for economic gain. The issue is when you release a monster like me on innocent people who are trying to obtain the dreams that my brothers and sisters have laid their lives on the line for."

"If you are wondering why I'm doing this, why I'm leaving this information for the world to see, it's because I did everything. I gave up everything." Tears started to roll down his face. "I proudly gave up my life to defend the American dream, not to suppress it."

Silas took a deep breath, and then with more urgency, he said, "Love, without knowing it, I had all the information in the world at my fingertips but allowed myself to be completely blind. I sentenced him to death for a handshake agreement."

Jessica was fully captivated. Silas continued, "Please forgive—" Then the door to the office flew open, and Michelle burst in, out of breath. "I think you'd better get out of here."

Jessica was caught completely off guard. "What are you talking about?"

"There are a couple of dark SUVs that I don't recognize coming up the road. You should leave out the back and take this." She handed Jessica a business card. It looked familiar, but Jessica didn't have time to analyze it. Jessica quickly gathered all of her things. As Michelle was ushering her toward the back of the house, she said, "After the rumors started about Silas, this woman came to visit me. She was the one who gave me the envelope. She told me that if I ever needed anything, to give her a call. Good luck."

Jessica ran out the back door and climbed the brick wall. As she lowered herself into the neighbor's yard, she saw the SUVs pulling up in front of Michelle's house. "*I gotta lay low,*" she thought to herself.

Luckily, Jessica had parked near the Stillmans' and walked over. She carefully made her way back to her car, jumped in, and quickly drove out of the neighborhood. Jessica pulled up to the intersection where she would turn left for her hotel. Instead, she turned right and headed toward the highway that went to the Huachuca Mountains that border Mexico. After driving for thirty minutes, she pulled off on a dirt road and continued for another ten miles. She makes a series of turns down a maze of dirt roads until she dead-ended at a manufactured home with no other house in sight. She knocked on the door, and a bubbly, youthful woman with long, dark hair, freckles, and a bright smile answered.

"Hey, Janice," Jessica said.

Chapter 44

"Hey, Jessica, this is a surprise," Janice said with excitement. "What are you doing here?"

"Yeah, I'm here for work, and something just, um, brought me to your door. Can I come in?" Jessica asked, trying to be discreet as she glanced over her shoulder. Jessica turned back to notice Janice looking past her as well.

"C'mon in! You're safe here," Janice said with a wink and a smile. She held the door open and waited for Jessica to come inside, ready to close the door behind her.

"So, you are here doing some work, huh?" Janice asked as she grabbed a couple of glasses from the cabinets and filled them with water.

"Yeah, just doing some research," Jessica replied. She accepted one of the glasses of water from Janice. "Thank you. And I'm actually hoping you won't mind if I just hole up in a corner and do a little work."

"You're welcome," Janice said. "And sure, feel free to research whatever, or whoever, for as long as you need."

"Is Atu coming home soon? I don't want to be in the way," Jessica said.

"Oh, don't worry about Atu. His brother is moving out here, so he went to go help him load up. His brother's a pack rat, so it'll probably take a while," Janice said.

Jessica made herself at home. She quickly opened her laptop and powered it on. She dumped out all the contents on the desk next to her computer, trying to decide where to start. "I think I'm missing something," she said underneath her breath.

"What makes you think that?" Janice asked.

"Oh," Jessica looked up, startled. "I didn't realize I said that out loud. I was saying that there's something that I must not be getting. Or there's something on these files that I missed."

"Why do you think that?" Janice asked.

"Someone in a black SUV seems to have tracked me. I swear I wasn't being followed, and the car appeared at Michelle's house after I accessed this SD card that someone left. I don't want to put you in any danger; I just needed to get off the grid quickly."

"Hey, you know that I'm still in your debt. If it weren't for your writing that corruption article, Atu still wouldn't be able to pursue his dream."

That was why Jessica did what she did. In her own way, she helped change arbitrary, biased rules that made it significantly more difficult for people of color to become business owners. *What I do matters,* she thought to herself, with a surge of determination.

"I couldn't let that stand without exposing it," Jessica said.

"We appreciate it. Wait," Janice said with growing fascination, "were you at Michelle Lukwago's house?"

Jessica responded slowly, eyeing Janice with curiosity, "Yes . . ."

"Are you doing a piece about the Hometown Hero, Silas?"

"Janice, I don't think —" Jessica said, looking around the house as if someone had bugged it.

"Don't worry, girl," Janice said. "I've already told you that you're safe here. No one finds this place unless we want them to."

Jessica looked Janice in the eye. "You can't tell anyone what I'm working on. There's an anonymous source who's paying my company a lot of money for this piece."

"Don't worry; your secrets are safe with me. We've been best friends since the second grade. When have I ever let one of your secrets slip?" Janice asked.

"Never," Jessica said, as she relaxed. "I don't know what's gotten into me. I've written articles that have pissed people off before, and that's okay. But it's one thing when it happens in some random city; it's another when someone strange follows me to the town I grew up in . . . You know?"

"Yeah, I hear you," Janice said as she finished assembling a couple of plates of food. She placed the plates down on the table and said with a laugh, "This sounds like something from a movie. What if someone was just watching Michelle's home?"

"But what would be so suspicious about me visiting Michelle?" Jessica asked.

"Well, did you visit the Stillman's house as well?" Janice asked, and Jessica nodded.

"How many visitors do you think both of those homes have gotten since Silas was publicly shamed?" Janice asked. "Especially from someone who hasn't lived here in years. If it was the feds or something, I'm sure that they already have what's in those folders."

"You're probably right. It all just seems odd for a case so many years old," Jessica said.

"And why are you looking into it again?" Janice asked. "Who do you think is cutting the check?"

Jessica ran scenarios through her mind and then realized that she was fidgeting with the card that Michelle handed her. She looked down at it again and realized that it matched the one from the folder M had given her. It was odd that in a matter of a couple of days, she had received two of the same card, especially a cryptic one with nothing but a phone number. Hesitantly, Jessica picked up her phone and dialed the number on the business card. The phone rang until Jessica heard the operator say, "The inbox for this number has not been set up. Please try your call again later." Jessica hung up the phone and debated whether to redial the number.

Just then, Jessica's phone buzzed, and she had a new e-mail from M. In the e-mail, there was an electronic airline ticket in Jessica's name, as well as an address. The message read, "The sponsor realized that there's one more person you need to speak with. Your name and all your credentials have been registered, so you shouldn't have any problems getting the appropriate access."

"Nebraska?" Jessica gasped. "Who do I need to see in Nebraska?"

Chapter 45

Jessica parked in an empty parking lot outside of a single-story building that looked like it used to be a bank. She double-checked the address. "Yes, this is definitely the place," she said to herself. It was a concrete building with slivers of dark windows that made it difficult to see inside. Jessica surveyed the area for any signs of life. The building was surrounded by cornfields, except for the one road that she drove there on.

Jessica made sure her recorder and notebook were in her bag and then hopped out of the car and approached the black glass doors. The doors were locked, so she tried to get a look inside by cupping her hands around her eyes and pressing her forehead against the door. As soon as her skin touched the glass, she heard a loud click and felt some sort of bolt unhinging. The door opened an inch or so. Jessica cautiously pushed the door open and stepped inside. She was surprised to see two heavily armed guards dressed in all black riot gear, standing on either side of the entrance hall. The guards were wearing black ski masks so you could only see their eyes, and neither of them acknowledged Jessica's presence. As soon as the door closed behind her, the next set of double doors opened.

As Jessica walked through, she saw at least ten more heavily armed guards manning posts throughout the inside of the building. She also noticed a very intense-looking metal detector. The guard tasked with operating the machine stuck his hand out, still not saying anything, motioning for her to place her bag on the table. After successfully passing through his checks, Jessica noticed that there was one guard standing in the middle of the spacious room in front of her. He seemed to be waiting on Jessica. As she approached him, she finally started to question, clearly a little too late, how safe this was and if she would ever be seen again.

Jessica started to speak, "Hi, my name is —"

Before she could finish, the guard interrupted her, "Jessica Ifill. We know who you are, ma'am. We've been ordered to take you to see our visitor. Please follow me." The guard turned around and led her past now-unused bank teller stations. They reached the old, giant bank vault. The guard entered a seven-digit numeric password on a pad next to the round metal door, lowered his head for a retina scan, and opened the vault.

"Why do you have so much security?" Jessica asked.

"It's to keep our guest comfortable," the guard said. "Now, please, ma'am, save the rest of your questions for our guest."

Inside the vault, four more armed soldiers were protecting what looked like an elevator door.

There's no way that's an elevator, Jessica thought. There was only one floor to this building.

Sure enough, it was, in fact, an elevator door that took them down at least a few stories underground. The elevator doors opened to a long concrete hallway, lit only by singular light bulbs encased in a protective wire hanging from the ceiling. Jessica stepped off the elevator, and the guard who escorted her did not follow. There were, however, two other guards standing outside of the elevator. They said nothing and did not move, so she started walking the only direction possible. The hallway stretched for a hundred meters, ending where two additional guards were positioned by the only door she had seen.

"Uh," Jessica said, "this is me?"

One of the guards replied, "We have been instructed to give you as much privacy as you need." With that, the guard opened the door. "You have one hour."

Jessica peered inside the room and, to her surprise, it was brightly lit, and the ceiling and remaining walls were a thick glass. The room had a toilet and a sink in one corner and a bookcase next to a neatly made bed in another corner. In the middle of the room was a table with two chairs. But what was incredible were the surroundings. She looked up at the ceiling, and it looked like she was staring directly at the beautiful blue sky with clouds slowing moving and shifting. The walls looked out on the cornfields as if they were sitting right in the midst of them.

"How is this possible?" Jessica asked. "Didn't I—"

"Travel a few stories below ground?" a man's voice finished her thought.

Jessica was so captivated by the room that she did not even notice the man standing along the sidewall.

"Hello, Jessica," the man said. "I'm sure that you have a lot of questions about a lot of things. We don't have much time, so we should be mindful of how we spend it." The man motioned toward one of the chairs, inviting Jessica to take a seat.

Jessica observed the man closely. He was tall and fit, with blue eyes and a long beard. His hair was neatly trimmed, and he was dressed in a gray sweat suit. He was older than she remembered, but she recognized him. "Holy shit. Silas Stillman?"

The man extended his hand. "I appreciate you making the trip to come and speak with me."

Caught off guard, Jessica shook his hand and stammered as she collected her thoughts, "Do— do you mind if I record this?"

"Please, go ahead," Silas said.

His voice was polite yet authoritative. Jessica could tell that this man was accustomed to giving unquestioned orders.

"Where do we start?" Silas asked, prompting her.

"Um," Jessica shook her head, snapping her thoughts into focus, "how about we start from the beginning. Tell me about yourself."

"My name is Silas Stillman," he started. "I grew up in a military town surrounded by the mountains. My dad owned a small business, and my mom had several jobs throughout my childhood. She took on any work that would help make ends meet. I received an athletic scholarship after high school, which led me to leave my hometown. Upon graduating, I served in the military for several years, traveling all over the world. I joined the military because I wanted to bring the freedom that I enjoyed here to every corner of the world where freedom and liberties were being taken away from people. I was a small-town kid with small-town ideals."

"I actually grew up in the same neighborhood as you," Jessica told him.

"So, you understand," he said. "Growing up in a small town, it's easy to see the world in a limited way. My ideologies were based on the inputs from a small number of people when you think about how vast and diverse the world is. And we lived in a military town, with people from various backgrounds." Silas coughed, then cleared his throat. "My apologies."

In a volume slightly louder than his conversational voice, Silas said, "Water, please."

"As I was saying," he continued, "once I had the opportunity to travel the world with the military, I began to lose that small-town thinking. I started to understand that many of the things I thought were true were a collection of lies. I came to realize that most things were done for economic reasons. Surprisingly, I was okay with it. I learned that, as an advanced civilization, wars weren't fought for people's rights or for land. Not really. They are fought over what can be produced by the land. It's about the economy, trade, and money. Commerce runs the world." Silas paused as one of the guards walked in with a pitcher of water, two glasses, and a bowl of fruit.

"Would you like any?" Silas asked, nodding to fruit as he poured them each a glass of water.

"No, I'm okay," Jessica responded, suppressing a laugh at the absurdity of the service provided for what seems to be a maximum-security prison for one man.

"Where was I?" Silas asked himself after the guard left. "Oh yes, the perception of economic stability in any country keeps the people at bay. This leads to peace. So, then I became okay with it. America has been one of the best countries in the world at providing this economic stability, and I was honored to do my best to progress any and every effort that would spread stability and peace around the world."

"You have a pretty impressive military record," Jessica said. "While most of the files I was given were heavily redacted, it was still plain to see that you've been a part of critical government missions, though you clearly landed in some controversy toward the end of your career. Is this how you justified your actions?"

Silas ignored her real question and continued, "People quickly forget how economic instability seems to be a precursor to tumbling nations. I knew from my studies of world history and have witnessed firsthand that when the masses feel hopeless and poor and when the wealthy do nothing to alleviate that feeling, chaos is soon to follow."

Silas started to eat some of the strawberries, blueberries, and pomegranate seeds. "Are you sure you don't want anything?"

"No, I'm good," Jessica said.

"After being successful in the field, our unit started working on international joint task force units. We busted large mob families, drug kingpins, and tyrants. I think since I looked the part, I started to get noticed from some suits in Washington. I was offered a job identifying people stateside who were weakening our democracy. I didn't want to leave my unit, but they were in capable hands. Luke was a great leader."

"Was that Christian Lukwago?" Jessica asked.

"That's right, he was my best friend and a damn fine American," Silas said beaming with pride. Then his expression shifted to sadness. "After I took my new job, my entire former unit was killed as part of a raid gone terribly wrong. Word was that Luke and the boys received bad intel and walked into an ambush." Silas took a long drink and his eyes watered; he was still impacted by the loss of his friends. "After that, I decided to put all of my energy, my entire being, into stopping anyone on US soil who was a threat to our democracy."

"Can you tell me how you are connected with the death of Ori Clayborn?" Jessica asked.

"Last I heard, they never found a body," Silas said, raising an eyebrow. "Has that changed?"

"No, it has not," Jessica responded, narrowing her eyes. "Can you please tell me how you are associated with the *disappearance* of Ori Clayborn?"

"That's better," Silas said with a smile, but didn't continue.

Jessica waited for a few more moments, then tried another approach. "Silas, can you tell me about the day that Ori was believed to have been killed?"

Silas smiled a sly smile. "I could tell you about that day, but . . ." he paused, "I think that you would find it more interesting to learn what happened three days prior."

Jessica looked at him skeptically.

"If you entertain me and let me tell you about three days before, then I will tell you what happened that day," Silas bargained.

Jessica considered this and then nodded in agreement.

Chapter 46

"As you've already discovered, I was working for a very covert government organization chartered with identifying and mitigating risks to our democracy. I was born to defend my country. I was proud of that promotion and felt like all my demanding work paid off. I believed in my heart that what I was doing was the right thing to do. And in the beginning, it was clear that the people we were going after were doing terrible things. We always found the trail and caught our person," Silas said, raising his pointer finger in the air.

"But Ori . . ." Silas said in slight admiration. "We couldn't find anything incriminating on Ori. Or, not at first, I should say."

"How did he come up on your radar?" Jessica asked.

"There was a politician who had a lot of pull. He claimed that Ori could be a person of interest and that we should look into him." Silas paused, choosing his words. "The unspoken assumption seemed to be that this was a very wealthy black guy who appeared out of nowhere, so there must be something there. However, we didn't find anything. It became an obsession for the higher-ups, and over time, we had our entire department trying to find everything we could about this guy. He was like a ghost. There was no school record, no criminal record, nothing. It was like he just manifested into existence out of thin air."

"That is hard to believe in this digital age," Jessica said.

"I absolutely agree. It made this case even more peculiar. To be honest," Silas said, looking down in shame, "that is where my logic left me and my ego kicked in. I became just as determined as the higher-ups to prove that he was guilty of something, or at least that he was a threat. I figured if we laid out the perfect trap for him and he took it, then he'd show us what he was hiding."

"Is that how you came up with the Wesley Corporation deal?" Jessica asked.

"That actually fell into our lap," Silas said. "I was thinking something boring like getting him caught up with a call girl, but he never took the bait. Then the FBI brought us a criminal informant whose girlfriend was working for Ori's company. They gave us some records that they claimed were proof of embezzlement, but they weren't solid. By the time the Wesley Corporation deal was brought to us by the FBI, I was so fixated on nailing this guy that I just ran with it without really thinking about what we were doing."

"So how does this relate to three days before Ori went missing?" Jessica asked.

"Okay, we can skip to that," Silas replied. "As you know, everyone was looking for Ori, and he just up and vanished. He could have been anywhere in the world. He was wealthy enough to hide out and buy a new identity, never to return. But, three days before the night of his disappearance, I got a couple of visitors at my cabin in Virginia."

"Ori?" Jessica asked.

"No, it was two men who were affiliated with Ori. One introduced himself as Tony, and the other one never gave a name. He was a big guy, a mountain with tribal tattoo sleeves. I would guess that he was from somewhere in the Polynesian Triangle. I tried to put up a fight, but they outmanned me. They restrained me, and then Tony took out a phone, dialed a number and put it on the table in front of me. It was Ori on the other end."

"What did he have to say?" Jessica asked, leaning forward.

"He told me what really happened to my old unit. He then walked me through the evidence on the harm my department was doing for the advancement of the American people. He asked me to join his team. I, of course, said no. I refused, at first, to believe anything that he was saying and told him so. Ori's response was kind of shocking."

"How so?" Jessica asked.

"I thought that he would have threatened me in some way, but instead, he said he understood. He said, 'Why would you trust me? You've been working to prove I'm everything that I'm not.' But what happened next gave me the chills."

Silas began telling the story as if he was living in it again.

"Ori said, 'I understand, Silas. Now, I hope you don't mind if I tell you what will happen next.'

"I said, 'I don't care what you do. Plus, it doesn't look like I have a choice.'

"He said that it was, unfortunately, necessary until I said everything that needed to be said. He told me, 'Tomorrow, two agents you know well from the FBI will seek you out. They will tell you that they have a strong confirmation of where I will be and that you will need to go with them back to Atlanta at once. Once in Atlanta, they will take you to a North Georgia forest.' Then he said, 'Here are the exact coordinates if you'd like,' and the big guy handed me a small strip of paper with some coordinates on it.

"Ori kept going, 'You'll arrive at that location a little after three thirty in the morning. It will be dark, and there will be a trail that leads to an old, abandoned shack. Rather than leave the car, you will be asked to wait in the vehicle with the two other agents. A second vehicle will arrive about an hour or so later. Don't panic. That will be a vehicle with a well-known political representative and yours truly. They will claim that they are waiting there with me until an extraction team comes to take me to a safe house, where I will wait until the trial or until this situation is cleared up.' But then Ori told me, 'I'm sure you can guess how this is really meant to end.'

"I remember telling him that I didn't want to hear all his nonsense, but that, of course, did not deter him.

"He kept telling me his prediction. 'They'll ask you to stay in the car until the two other agents from our vehicle have checked and cleared the shack. Then they'll move me.'

"Ori became extremely intent that I pay close attention after this. He told me, 'Once the two agents are back in the car, one of the agents who drove you to this location will take out his firearm and kill those men. Silas, you mustn't react. If you do, they will turn their firearm on you next. They will ask you in some way if you are truly ready to earn your seat at the big boy's table. When you go into the shack, they will expect you to shoot me. When you see me sitting in the chair, pull out your firearm immediately, turn off the safety, and aim it at my chest.'"

"Hang on," Jessica interrupted. "Ori told you this three days before it happened?"

"Yes," Silas said. "And it played out exactly as he predicted it would."

"Why would he tell you all of this?" Jessica asked.

"Just wait, it gets better." Silas launched back into his tale.

"Once Ori told me that I would be asked to shoot him, the big guy with the tattoos pulled out a firearm that looks exactly like the one I carry.

"Ori kept talking as if able to see what was happening in the room. 'This gun has special blanks. If you decide to join us and do the right thing, then use this firearm instead of your own.'

"'And if I don't?' I asked.

"Ori's reply was so calm and matter of fact. He said, 'Then use your firearm and kill me. I've just told you the future, Silas; you decide what to do with it.'

"I asked him, 'Why would I betray my country for you?'

"'You're betraying your country with what you are doing now, not with what you should be doing with us,' was his reply.

"'This would be treason,' I said. I was genuinely trying to wrap my head around what he was telling me and the choices laid out in front of me.

"'We need to prepare for something much bigger than squabbles among men,' Ori said.

"The big guy placed the pistol on my counter, Tony picked the phone back up, and they left. They couldn't have known which one I would actually use."

Silas took a drink of water and locked eyes with Jessica. "One more thing was really interesting. Ori told me not to worry and that I wouldn't have to pull the trigger."

"What?" Jessica's brow furrowed with confusion.

Silas continued, "He said that the senator would want to do it, so be prepared to hand the gun over to him." Silas paused. "Then he said that it was important that after the senator pulled the trigger, I needed to quickly take the pistol back." Silas laughed and shook his head in amazement. "I can hear his voice like he just told this to me yesterday. 'At exactly four thirty-seven a.m., someone will burst into the door of that shack, and it must be you, Silas, who pulls the trigger.'"

"Was Ori right?" Jessica asked.

"About which part?" Silas asked.

"Everything that Ori told you, did it come true?" Jessica asked.

"Again, down to the tiniest detail," Silas said.

"So, you are telling me that Ori predicted the night of his death, or disappearance, in full detail, three days prior?" Jessica asked.

"That's correct," Silas confirmed.

"Why would he walk into that? Especially not knowing which gun you'd choose. With the means he had, why turn himself over?" Jessica asked.

"I asked him that same question," Silas said. "He said it was time to move into the next phase of his mission."

"Which was what?" Jessica asked skeptically.

"Not for me to say," answered Silas. "But he did give me one more prediction that I didn't mention yet."

"And what was that?" Jessica couldn't believe there was more.

"Ori told me that if I made the right choice, that one day, I could tell my story. But he gave me stipulations. He told me that, one day, I would read some impressive articles by a young journalist. When that happens, she is the one that I should share this story with, and no one until then. And even then, I should wait until I feel like the time is right to give my permission to make it public."

"Ori told you about me?" Jessica asked.

"Yes, he did," Silas nodded.

"But—" Jessica started, confounded. "Who am I, and what role do I play in all of this?"

"I don't know, but aren't you intrigued to find out?"

Jessica remained quiet for a moment, her mind racing. Finally, realizing her time must be ending, she decided to get just a couple more answers. "So, you're my anonymous client. And the guards kept referring to you as a guest or a visitor. What are you doing here? It's pleasant, but isn't it still a prison?"

"You're right, but it's a prison of my own design. I'm here by choice. A debt has to be repaid — a life for a life," Silas said.

"Your life for Ori's life?" Jessica asked.

"Ha, you still don't get it." Silas shook his head. "My life for Christian's life. It's my fault he is dead. I was blind and ambitious, and I lost my way. I sacrificed Christian, unknowingly, but I did it nevertheless. For that, I'm okay spending the rest of my life confined. The one thing I do want, which has been granted to me, is that the remaining people who matter to me can one day know the truth."

"Which is?" prompted Jessica.

Silas moved to the wall and touched the glass pane. "Home," he whispered gently. A video of Michelle came up on the screen. But it was of a different, much younger Michelle. She was smiling at the screen as if it was a home video.

"What is this?" Jessica asked.

"It's an old memory," Silas said, "of better, happier days."

Without looking back at Jessica who was still sitting at the table, Silas whispered, "Our hour is up. Thank you for your visit, Ms. Ifill."

As soon as the word *Ifill* left Silas's lips, the door to the prison cell opened. Two guards appeared, ready to escort Jessica out.

"One last thing," Silas said, still staring at the memory displayed on the wall. "Ori told me that if I took the pistol that he left, then I would be granted a gift of sight." Silas turned his head and made eye contact with her. "Once you have this gift for seeing the truth, you're never able to go back," he said just before the door closed.

Chapter 47

Jessica walked out of the concrete building and squinted as she tried to reacclimate to the Nebraska sunshine. Jessica always took a moment after interviewing incarcerated people to breathe in the fresh air and appreciate her circumstances in life. Your freedom is not something to take for granted.

Jessica exhaled and started walking toward her rental car when a large, black SUV pulled up to her side. The passenger side doors swung open, and two men in dark suits stepped out quickly. Without saying a word to her, they blocked her exit so that the only direction Jessica could go was into the SUV's back seat.

"Please get in," a woman said from across the back seat. She was looking down at some documents in her lap. "We won't hurt you. We just want to talk."

Jessica climbed into the back, eyeing the woman cautiously. She recognized her as Deputy Director Mikiko Shikibu of the FBI. Jessica had read up on her not long ago for a different story.

"So, Ms. Ifill," the deputy director said, "we have been monitoring Silas's closest family and friends since the incident. They have been understandably guarded, and then you come along, and they just talk."

"What do you want?" Jessica asked.

"Are you writing a piece on this?" Deputy Director Shikibu asked, motioning down at the manila file in her lap.

"I'm not at liberty to say," Jessica said.

"How was your time with Silas?" the deputy director asked.

"Why do you care?" Jessica retorted.

Deputy Director Shikibu tilted her head, sizing up Jessica. "Evelyn was my best friend in the world and my hero. I don't believe the story that they told us. The idea that La Tiniebla Cartel did a hit and was in the middle of cleaning up their mess before the ambulance scared them off never held water with me. From what we know, La Tiniebla doesn't let people off that easily. They don't just pick off a couple of people in a room full of agents." Mikiko Shikibu looked back to her stack of papers. "I've read your work, and I know you are a straight shooter. You do the right thing. You do great research, and you draft your stories as they happened. So, what I want is to talk to you. I want to tell you my part, and I hope that it helps you find the truth."

"There's a coffee shop a few miles up the road," the deputy director said. "The coffee is terrible, but it will be a quiet place to talk."

Once there, they chose a table and ordered some coffee. The service was quick since they were the only souls there. Jessica pulled out her recorder. "So, tell me what you remember."

Deputy Director Shikibu took a sip of her coffee and then began. "Agent Cramer was speeding down the highway with the sirens blaring. It was in the middle of the night, fortunately, so there were no drivers on the road. We had twenty squad cars following us, with officers from the local city and county police precincts in Georgia. I was shouting the coordinates to a dispatcher so that an ambulance could be sent preemptively." She squinted her eyes as if the tighter she closed them, the more vivid the images of the past would appear.

"We were fortunate that there was an ambulance available and close by. They were the first responders on the scene. They saw some vehicles fleeing the other way when they arrived, but they didn't see any faces and weren't able to get a license plate number. When we arrived, the two medics had already gotten Ori into the back of the ambulance, and they were in the process of getting Evelyn up and in as well. Evelyn had on an oxygen mask and was weak. I was only able to see her for a moment, and it was difficult to understand her, but I swear she said, 'I'm sorry.' Then the medics got her in the ambulance and rushed them off to the hospital."

The deputy director looked down at her coffee. "And that was the last time I saw my friend alive."

Then she shook her head, snapping herself out of the sad thought. "But you aren't here for all of that. Let's see . . . When we arrived at the crime scene, there was a government-issued SUV there. Inside were Senator Whitman's guards, one shot in the forehead at point-blank range, and the other shot in his chest. Both had their weapons holstered. It looked like they were caught by surprise. The senator was unconscious in the back seat of the vehicle. He didn't remember a thing."

"How do you surprise two highly trained guards who are protecting a US senator? And a popular one at that," Jessica asked.

"I kept asking myself that same question. How do you get the drop on not one, but two, well-trained guards? They must have known the shooters, and probably pretty well, to allow them to get that close." Deputy Director Shikibu looked out of the window. "I've had my suspicions of who it could have been, but I was never able to prove it. And then he disappeared not long after as well."

She looked back at Jessica. "And unfortunately, that's all the evidence that I have."

Jessica thought for a minute. "There's nothing else you remember about that night? Why was Special Agent Blackwood there by herself?"

"I never figured that out," the deputy director said. "The deciphered text message said to come alone. It was such a stupid thing to do, and Evelyn was anything but stupid."

"I remember reading that she and Ori knew each other as kids," Jessica said.

"Yes," the deputy director said, "but there was never any indication that they knew each other well. We did do some more digging, but neither had any living family members. They were both only children whose parents had passed. We, of course, talked to each of their associates, but we didn't uncover anything that helped us understand what happened."

"So, there were no other solid leads at the crime scene?" Jessica asked.

"None. Have you uncovered anything?"

Jessica knew that the information she had was more than enough to give the deputy director some closure, but Jessica felt nervous that if she gave up this information, she would be breaching her contract. She decided to divert.

"Tell me about the medics," Jessica said.

"What do you mean?" Deputy Director Shikibu asked.

"What can you remember about them?" Jessica asked. "Did you do follow up interviews with them?"

"I never got the driver's name," the deputy director said, "but I was able to find the lead EMT. His name was Vavau Moe'uhane. He went by Vau."

Jessica was surprised. She said casually, "You remember that well."

Deputy Director Shikibu smiled. "He was memorable. Big guy, lots of tattoos. He said that he was originally from Samoa and that he hadn't been in Atlanta for very long. He said he didn't see anything, and he thought that the ambulance sirens scared off anyone who was still in the cabin."

"Did you ever see Vau again?" Jessica asked.

"I went back to the area to search the cabin for evidence again and decided to stop by the hospital. Vau wasn't there, and they said that he was taking his motorcycle on a trip across the country. I've never seen him since. I could have followed his trail, but I didn't see a reason to. So, I buried my head in my work."

"Here's what I can tell you," Jessica started. "I think that there's more to this story as well. I do have some information that will shed some light. I cannot tell you right now. If you really want to know what happened to your friend, then you are going to have to trust me on this. Please give me a little more time, and I will make sure to share everything I find with you. Deal?"

"I've waited this long to know what happened; I can wait a little longer." The deputy director shook Jessica's hand. "Deal."

"In the meantime . . .," Jessica paused, "can you do me one favor?"

"What's that?" the Deputy Director asked.

Jessica pulled the business card out of her pocket. "Can you have someone look this number up and let me know who it belongs to? I've tried calling it several times, and no one ever answers, and the voicemail isn't set up."

Deputy Director Shikibu studied the card and the number. "Where did you get this?"

"It was part of the packet of information that my boss gave me as research for this story. Why; do you recognize the number?" Jessica asked.

"Yes, I do, actually. I'm afraid you may not have much luck chasing down the owner though."

"Why is that?" Jessica asked.

"This number belongs—," Mikiko Shikibu corrects herself, "belonged to Jordan."

"Who's Jordan?" Jessica asked.

"She was Ori's assistant at the Singularity Group. After Ori went missing and Leslie took over, Jordan became kind of a recluse. It's exceedingly difficult to track her down. If anyone can get you close to Jordan, it will be Leslie. I wouldn't hold my breath though. No one has seen Jordan in a few years."

Chapter 48

Leslie heard two knocks on her office door. "Come in!" she called.

Her executive assistant walked into her office. "Your ten thirty meeting just arrived."

Leslie looked at her assistant and narrowed her eyes, trying to remember what meeting she had scheduled at ten thirty. "I thought that my next meeting was with the mayor at noon."

"It was, but it looked like you added this meeting to your calendar, and I couldn't decline or delete it."

"That's bizarre. Who is the meeting with?" Leslie asked.

"A lady named Jessica Ifill," her assistant said. "She says that she's a journalist from Str8 Truth Media in Washington, DC."

"Did she say what she wants?"

"She's here to talk to you about Jordan."

"You can send her in," Leslie said.

Jessica walked in and took a seat across from Leslie.

"Thank you for taking the time to see me," Jessica said. "I know how extremely busy you are running this massive company."

Leslie smiled politely. "How may I be of service?"

"I'm actually trying to locate someone who works here, or maybe used to work here." Jessica's face was inquisitive.

"You're looking for Jordan, correct?" Leslie asked, cutting to the chase.

"Yes!" Jessica's eyes flashed. "Does she still work here?"

"She does," Leslie said, but stopped there.

Jessica shifted in her seat and, after a moment, asked, "Can I speak to her?"

"May I ask why you wish to speak to her?" Leslie asked.

"I'm investigating the disappearance of Ori Clayborn. The information I've received so far keeps pointing me to Jordan," Jessica said, clearly trying to read Leslie's face. "I believe that Jordan is my best shot at understanding what happened to Ori."

"Why is that?" Leslie asked.

Jessica took out the two business cards and handed them to Leslie. "I've been given both of these over the past couple of days. I've tried to call, but no one ever answers or calls back. One of my sources told me that this is Jordan's number and that she hasn't been seen in a while."

Leslie placed her index finger on her cheek and rested her chin on her thumb. "Jordan does still work here, although it is tough to get hold of her. She leads special projects, which means that she travels quite a bit and can come and go as needed."

Jessica looked down and exhaled audibly. Leslie could tell she was a bit deflated.

"The good news," Leslie continued, "is that Jordan is due to show up soon. She's pretty dependable about following up, so if you want to leave me your contact information, I can make sure that she gets it."

"That would be great," Jessica said eagerly and handed a business card to Leslie. "While I'm here, may I ask you a few questions about Ori and the Singularity Group?"

"Of course," Leslie said. "No one has asked me about Ori in years."

"I've read the notes from the investigation, and next to Jordan, it sounds as if you may have worked most closely with Ori. Is that correct?" Jessica asked.

"Yes, that is correct."

"He must have really trusted you to hand over his entire company to you. Do you know why he did this?" Jessica asked.

"He thought that I was best equipped to continue with his plan," Leslie responded.

"Which was what, exactly?"

"To run the business in a way that puts our stakeholders first." Leslie's chin tipped up with pride. "As a privately held company, our stakeholders are our employees, customers, partners, and the communities that we serve.

He wanted stable growth and expansion, but never at the risk of our stakeholders."

"Singularity Group has been facing more competition in your lending and franchise business units lately. How have you been able to maintain such a strong level of growth?" Jessica asked.

"People only tend to focus on those two aspects of our business, but they don't really understand that we are very diverse. The Singularity Group has a wide array of subsidiaries, many of which have countless patents that we license out to major companies around the world."

"Really?" Jessica's eyebrows raised. "I hadn't heard that."

"Yes," Leslie assured her. "Ori firmly believed that the core purpose of each human being was to create. He would often say that we are all creators of something, and once you allow people the freedom to do what we were designed to do, then the possibilities are limitless."

"He sounds like he was an admirable man," Jessica said.

"Yes, very," Leslie responded. "So, I would imagine that you have read the statement that I gave to the FBI the night Ori went missing?"

"I did," Jessica nodded, "but . . ." she paused.

"But what?" Leslie asked, with a sly smile.

"Can I speak plainly? I don't want to cause any offense," Jessica said.

"Go ahead. I don't offend easily," Leslie responded.

"Your statement didn't really make sense to me."

"Why not?" Leslie asked.

"Well," Jessica looked down at her hands briefly, trying to think of the right words. "Your statement says that after the explosion, you were checked out by the physician's assistant on staff. Then, you attended an interview with Ori and the FBI before escaping the building with Ori." Jessica paused to flip through her notepad. "And then you proceeded to a secluded island with Ori, Jordan, and Tony where you met with someone named Professor Raziel."

"That's correct," Leslie said, still with a sly smile on her face.

"But," Jessica's forehead creased, "I have also read from several reports that you were taken to the hospital immediately following the explosion and that you were in a coma the entire time between the explosion and the incident leading to Ori's disappearance."

"Go on," Leslie said.

"I also read the FBI transcripts, and they, too, say that you were not present when they questioned Ori," Jessica said. "There's no record of a Professor Raziel, and no one has been able to locate Tony."

"Now comes the billion-dollar question," Leslie said. "Do you believe me? Have there been any other anomalies in what you've read?"

"The FBI did confirm that your cell phone was on the plane that they searched in the Virgin Islands."

"Was there anything else?" Leslie asked.

Jessica tilted her head, looking up and to the left, deep in thought. Then she looked back to Leslie and asked, "How did you get from the senator's house to the hospital?"

"How do you think?" Leslie asked.

"In your statement, you said that Ori called a friend to pick you up from Senator Lane Whitman's house when everything was safe. You described the massive man as being of Polynesian descent with tattoo arm sleeves."

"Yes, that was Vau," Leslie said. "He, too, is a good friend of Ori's."

"What time did he pick you up?" Jessica asked, now leaning forward in her chair.

"Sometime after nine o'clock in the morning," Leslie said, now leaning back in her chair.

The room was silent as Jessica tried to wrap her head around this detail that she missed. Who was Vau? How did he know Ori?

Leslie's assistant stepped into the office. "Ben and Angie are asking if you have a few minutes. They have something set up in conference room one that they'd like a quick reaction to." Leslie looked out of the glass window to see a couple of associates peering into her office with curiosity. Leslie said, "Privacy, please," and the glass walls converted to a frosty opaque color.

Leslie told her assistant, "Tell them I'll be right there."

Leslie then turned to Jessica. "I'd like to continue this conversation if you have a few more minutes."

"Of course, I would love that," Jessica replied.

"Great!" Leslie smiled. "It's been so long since . . ." she paused. "You know, this used to be Ori's office. After he left, I tried to make it my own, but I didn't have the heart to remove everything. I kept a few of his photos. Feel free to take a look around. I'll be back in a few minutes."

Chapter 49

Jessica was looking around Leslie's office and noticed a framed picture of Ori with a group of people. They were all smiling, as if one of them told a funny joke right before the picture was taken. *Are these Ori's friends?* Jessica thought to herself. It looked like the photo was taken on a hike or trek through the jungle.

In the picture, everyone had machetes with leather sheaths. They looked similar to the way people were dressed when she was backpacking through Central America. It always struck Jessica that parts of the world still use machetes to do things like cut grass or work in the fields. This photo also struck her because it was the only clue that Ori was ever in a relationship or that he had friends outside of Jordan and Leslie.

Jessica saw a petite woman who was trying her best to keep a straight face. Jessica recognized Ori, of course, whose pose caught Jessica off guard. He was standing there, smiling ear to ear, with a woman hugging him around the neck and kissing him on the cheek. You couldn't get a view of her face, almost as if she was intentionally hiding it. The way Ori's arm was around her lifted her shirt up and exposed her skin up to her ribcage. Jessica also recognized Tony. There was a picture of him in the file she was given by M.

Leslie walked back into the office. "That's a great photo, right?"

"Who are all of these people?" Jessica asked, looking closely at all of the faces. "The FBI said that they couldn't track down anyone else who knew Ori well." Jessica paused as she felt her pulse quicken. "The tattoo sleeve . . ." she said. "Is that Vau?"

"Yep, and that's Jordan," Leslie said, pointing to the petite woman. Leslie looked at Jessica intently. "Do you still think I made up my statement?"

"Quite honestly, I don't know what to think," Jessica said.

"That's fair, but hopefully with time, you'll figure it out. Listen, I've got to run and take care of something. Keep looking around if you want. I'll trust that you will see yourself out when you are ready." Leslie began to leave the office while Jessica sat on the couch studying the picture.

"Wait," Jessica said quickly, before Leslie left.

"Yes?" Leslie paused and turned around.

"How long have you had this photo?"

"It's been here for as long as I've been sitting in the office. Ori had it on his desk while he was here. Why do you ask?" Leslie asked.

"Have you ever taken the picture out of the frame?" Jessica asked.

"No, I haven't. And I think only Ori and Jordan ever really touched the photo." Leslie's eyebrows raised. "Did you find something interesting?"

"I think so, but it could also be a crazy coincidence," Jessica said hesitantly.

"I don't believe in coincidences anymore. Feel free to take that photo with you if you think that it will be helpful."

"Really?" Jessica was surprised, but excited.

"I've been staring at that photo for a lot of years, and nothing has ever come to me. If it's speaking to you, then maybe that means something." Just like that, Leslie left the office.

Once Leslie left, Jessica looked even more closely at Ori's T-shirt. The shirt was almost completely drenched, but Jessica could just make out the writing. "The Defenders of Camelot," Jessica whispered, while touching the back of her neck.

Jessica opened the back of the picture frame to get a closer look at the photo. On the back of the photo, someone had written, "The Conception at Maderas."

Jessica grabbed her things and hurriedly fled the office. As soon as she was out of the building, she called M. "Hey, I think I found something. Can you make international travel arrangements for me, please?"

"Of course," M said. "Where are you going?"

"Ometepe, in Nicaragua," Jessica said.

Chapter 50

Jessica held up the picture to the taxi driver. "Seguro?" she asked. "Are you sure this is the place?"

"Sí, sí," the taxi driver said. "The man with the tattoos."

The taxicab had stopped at a dirt driveway, with a sign at the end that said, "Cabins for Rent."

As Jessica walked down the gravel driveway with her hiking pack on her back, she heard several voices and an eruption of laughter. It sounded like a happy group, all talking and laughing over each other. Jessica was getting close to the first cabin when she heard a woman's voice say, "I think I hear someone coming."

That voice was quickly followed by a second woman's voice. "We have company."

Jessica paused just around the corner. She heard the squeak of a screen door, and then a man's voice saying, "While you're up, will you get one for me and one for our guest as well, please?"

"Of course," the voice of the first woman said.

"C'mon, Jessica, now's not the time to be shy," the man said.

Jessica was filled with anticipation. She nodded her head as if he could see her and then turned the corner. There were several people sitting around a long, wooden table. She recognized Tony, Vau, and Jordan. Sitting at the head of the table was Ori. Directly next to him on both sides were open seats. Ori motioned to his right, inviting Jessica to sit down. Jordan gave her a friendly nod, and Jessica slowly approached the table. But as soon as Jessica sat down, everyone except for Ori stood up and left the table in unison.

"Welcome, Jessica. It was the T-shirt, right?" Ori said with a wide smile, displaying his bright teeth.

Jessica, now seated and facing him, marveled. "You haven't aged at all."

"Why, thank you," Ori said, head slightly cocked. "That's a compliment, right?"

A woman came back out and sat in the open seat to Ori's left. The woman had curly, strawberry-blonde hair that fell down to her shoulders. She had almond-shaped green eyes, and when she flashed Jessica a warm smile, they crinkled pleasantly. She handed Jessica a bottle of water and set an empty glass in front of her. "Would you like some wine?"

"You— you're Evelyn, I mean, Agent Blackwood, aren't you?" Jessica stammered. "What is going on? The world thinks you both are dead. What are you doing here?"

"Actually," Ori said, "we have been waiting for you."

"Wh— What are you talking about?" Jessica asked. Just then, Jordan, Tony, and Vau walked back nearby, wearing backpacks and hiking gear. They sat on the porch.

"We are getting ready to go on a hike, but we needed to speak with you first," Ori said. "We are thrilled that you figured it out when you did."

"Figured what out?" Jessica asked.

Evelyn interjected, "The T-shirt. Ori was so excited about that T-shirt. He knew that you would get it."

Ori said, "I had it made specifically so that you would recognize it."

"But how? I don't understand. That picture was taken at least a decade before I even thought about writing the article," Jessica said.

"Time is a funny thing, isn't it?" Ori then became serious. "I can't go into everything with you right now, but what I am going to tell you is very important. Do you understand?"

Jessica nodded her head slowly.

"We don't have very much time, and speaking right now goes against protocol. But, since I am here under extraordinary circumstances, I get to bend a few rules. First, thank you for accepting my invitation."

I don't know that I'd call it an invitation, Jessica thought to herself.

"Oh, but it was, designed specifically for you," Ori said out loud.

Jessica gasped, "Can you—"

"Read your thoughts? Yes, not that it's difficult at the moment, but we will get into that at another time," Ori said. "We have a grave request for you. We need someone to do unbiased reporting on the trial."

"Trial, what trial?" Jessica asked.

Ori continued, "There is a trial underway now, at the very highest of levels. Evelyn and I have been on a mission to prove that these people are worth saving. I believe that if we can bring this trial and the progress being made out into the light, for the public to witness, then there is a chance that we will win."

"Who are *these people* in this scenario?" Jessica asked.

Evelyn placed her hand on Ori's forearm. "Jessica," she said, her voice calm, "this is a trial unlike any before and will be unlike any after. This is a trial that could determine the fate and future of all you know."

"What?" Jessica exclaimed. "This sounds extreme."

"I know this may be a lot to digest." Ori looked back at Jessica. "Think about it like this: The universe is a living thing, and just like any other living thing, its objective is to grow and expand. The Earth is meant to play a critical role in this universal expansion but can only do that when human beings do what they are meant to do. There was a time when Earth was marvelous. However . . .," Ori paused, "let's just say that, currently, there is a lot of room for improvement. And what happens on Earth can cause a ripple effect throughout the universe."

"I suppose that sounds like it could be true," Jessica said thoughtfully. "Things have been getting better over the past few years though."

"And you've already started to write about these changes, which is exactly what we need," Ori said. "Things were bleak for so long that a total reset was being considered. Fear, violence, ego, and war were running rampant. An advocate proposed that if we were able to confine those negative forces, then Earth and its people could get back on the right track. We," Ori motioned to his group of friends, "have been charged with carrying out this task."

"And what is the right track?" asked Jessica, her head swimming.

"Every individual has greatness in him. The right track is when people are pursuing that greatness and not allowing these destructive energies and efforts to derail them."

"Okay . . ." Jessica thought for a moment. "Let's say that what you are telling me is true. Who will be the judge? How do you win a trial with the universe?"

"You collect as much consistent evidence as possible to support that Earth is still a beacon of light," Ori said.

"What does that kind of evidence look like?" Jessica asked.

"The only evidence that the universe cares about is people like you: people doing what they are meant to do, what they were built to do." Ori looked at his watch. "My job is to recruit as many people as possible, people who want to do the right thing with the gifts that they've been granted. The more people we have, the greater the chances of winning. All I ask of you is to simply document what you witness. That's it."

"That's it?" Jessica asked skeptically. "Document what I witness?"

Ori raised an eyebrow and gave a lopsided smile. "Are you in?"

"Well, it just kind of sounds like my job. But tell me this," Jessica paused. "Who are you, really?"

"It's a bit complicated, but in the flesh, I'm the Ori that you see. But my soul, or my spirit, is . . ." Ori searched for the right words, then smiled. "It's something very different. Something older than time."

"So," Ori extended his hand, "if you choose to shake my hand, you're making a choice to document only what you witness. Nothing more, nothing less. And by shaking my hand, I will grant you the gift of sight. This will allow you to see what is at stake. Do you agree? Will you join us?"

"Oh, why not!" Jessica firmly grabbed and shook Ori's hand.

"Great," Evelyn said, clapping her hands. "We've got the record keeper."

"Now what?" Jessica asked as Jordan walked over with two hiking packs.

"Now, it's time for you to go home," Ori said as he took his bag from Jordan and put it on his back. He then helped Evelyn with hers.

"You guys ready?" Vau asked. "We've got to get going."

Ori nodded to Vau. Then he looked back at Jessica. "Jordan will take you back, and we will be in touch soon. If you need anything, you have Jordan's number." Vau and Tony started leading the way, with Ori and Evelyn close behind.

"Wait, that's it?" Jessica asked. She tried to follow them but was unable to move. Her feet seem to be glued to the ground. "What is happening? Why can't I move?"

Ori's group vanished out of sight, and Jordan leaned in a few inches from Jessica's face. Jordan whispered, "Close your eyes and remember your commitment."

Jessica, without thinking, followed Jordan's instructions. She felt Jordan's hands gently grasp her shoulders, and within a split second, her head jerked forward and then backward.

"Hey!" Jessica jumped up and looked around.

"Hey, are you okay?" Leslie's assistant asked.

"Where am I?" Jessica was bewildered.

The assistant pursed her lips. "Um, you are still in Leslie's office. You fell asleep on the couch."

Jessica tried to orient herself. "What? How long have I been asleep?"

"Only about fifteen minutes," the assistant said. "Also, Jordan's here and is ready to —"

Jordan interrupted the assistant as she walked into the room. "I've got it from here. Thank you." She looked at Jessica. "Are you okay?"

"My head, it's throbbing," Jessica said, blinking and rubbing her temples. "Why is it so bright in here?"

The assistant took her leave. Jessica tried to look at Jordan, but she felt like someone was flashing an insanely bright flashlight in her eyes. "Can you turn that off, please?"

Jordan laughed and stepped further into the office. "He gave you a gift of sight," Jordan said, and it sounded somewhere between a question and a statement. Before Jessica could answer, she added, "It will take a little bit to get used to, but you'll get the hang of it."

Jessica was at a loss for words for a moment. Then she told Jordan, "You are absolutely radiant."

Jordan let out another laugh. "You should take a look at yourself."

Jordan walked Jessica into the hidden bathroom on the side of the office, and they stood in front of the mirror.

"What is wrong with me?" Jessica asked, with slight panic. "Why am I glowing?"

"Your greatness is showing. This is what you're looking for," Jordan said.

Chapter 51

The Senator's SUV stopped at the edge of a forest clearing in the North Georgia mountains. The guard in the passenger seat looked back and said, "Let's hop out. We're walking from here." Ori stepped out of the back seat and stretched his arms over his head. He sensed motion behind him, and then everything went dark.

Ori came to in a dark room that he didn't recognize.

"Did you think we were going to let you get away with it?" The man's voice was both incredulous and triumphant. The light from the full moon began to fill the room as Ori's eyes adjusted. He inhaled deeply. The man continued as if he was talking to himself, "We knew you were up to something. Did you actually think that you stood a chance?" Ori surveyed the room. He squinted to focus on his surroundings.

"Are you listening to me?" the man continued speaking while Ori remained silent, not acknowledging him. Ori made out three bodies in the room with him: one talking, one holding a flashlight, and a third one close to what looked like the door.

The shack was an old cabin but was well built. No lights were turned on, nor was there a fire burning, so as not to attract any unwanted attention. The natural moonlight was perfect to illuminate most of the space. In the areas where the moonlight did not reach, there was the glow of a bright flashlight. This flashlight was suddenly pointed directly into Ori's eyes.

"Are you listening to me?" the man continued, his voice vaguely familiar.

"Can you help me understand what this is?" Ori asked. He then looked down at his arms. "Are handcuffs really necessary?"

"They're a precaution." The man continued, "And please don't play dumb. You know exactly what this is about."

Ori said, with a hint of attitude, "Oh, but I would really like to hear you explain why you're restraining me in a dingy shack in the middle of the woods. I've done nothing wrong."

"Your greed, Mr. Clayborn," a new voice said from behind him. Ori turned to see a shadowy figure move in the darkest corner in the cabin. "The technology that you are creating will revolutionize our entire existence. The wealth that could be created is unimaginable."

Ori let the man talk.

The shadowy figure continued, "Manipulating dark matter can bring us into a new era and secure the US's place as the biggest global powerhouse." The man, now inches away from Ori's ear, whispered loudly enough for everyone in the room to hear, "But you were unwilling to share the wealth."

"On the contrary," Ori said, "all I do is share the wealth with those who deserve it."

The first man jumped back in, ignoring what Ori said, "All you were asked to do was take your company public. Why you couldn't get with the program is beyond me."

"Oh, please, that's not what this is about," Ori scoffed. "Is this little show for the senator's benefit? Yes, I know you're here, Lane." Ori cast his eyes toward the man by the door.

"You're brave for someone who won't see the sunrise tomorrow," the first man said.

"That's big coming from someone who won't show his face," Ori said. "But, don't worry, I don't need you to, Agent Chivington."

That shut the man up.

"Silas," Ori continued, "enough with the light in my face." Then Ori tilted his head back and to the left. "You must be the notorious Section Chief Appleton."

The men were all silent. "Jeremy," Ori said, "we haven't officially met, but I feel like we know a lot about each other. The question I'd be asking myself if I were you is, who knows more? Do you know more about me, or do I know more about you?"

Agent Chivington started clapping. "That's an excellent trick. Silas, you were so eager to shoot him before. I think now's your time."

Silas pointed his gun at Ori's chest.

"Whoa, whoa," Lane finally spoke up. "It's not the time for that just yet, is it? Let's keep our heads."

"You brought him here," said Chivington. "Now let's hope you aren't having a change of heart. You do still want that Oval Office, don't you, Lane?"

"I've earned that already," said Lane heatedly.

"Oh, have you?" asked Section Chief Appleton condescendingly. "You should know, better than anyone, that nothing is guaranteed without the help of the powers that be. And now we need to see your dedication to the cause."

Lane glared at him, but looked like there was a battle within.

Then Agent Chivington chimed in again with a smooth, enticing voice. "With one small sacrifice, you will have everything you've ever dreamed of. You will become the leader of the Free World. All you have to do is put a stop to him."

The senator took a deep breath.

Chivington continued, "We know that you are the man, the only man, for the job. We know that you will get this nation back to its former glory. Only you can. But, you have to be willing to sacrifice."

"Silas, give me that gun," said Lane, with a determined edge to his voice.

Silas handed it over. Lane took aim at Ori and pulled the trigger.

But Ori was unaffected. Silas grabbed the gun back from the senator. The door to the shack flew open, and Silas fired at Agent Blackwood as she came through the door.

Then, in a low, clear voice, Ori said, "Don't move."

The four men all freeze in place against their will.

"That's better," Ori said with a smile.

Vau, Tony, and Jordan walk in behind Evelyn, who was standing tall and defiant.

"Can you please take these handcuffs off?" Ori said. None of Ori's friends make a move, but a bright flash of moonlight hit the handcuffs, and the metal fell to the floor. Ori stood up and rubbed his wrists.

"Who are you?" Chivington asked, eyes filled with fire.

"Hello, Ego," said Ori, looking Agent Chivington right in the eye. "You didn't sense this coming?"

After a few seconds, Chivington's eyes narrowed. "Impossible!"

"Why?" Ori asked. "Surely you knew your time here would need to come to an end."

Agent Chivington turned red with rage. "How dare you come here now, after all this time. To remove me?" he exclaimed, indignant. He breathed heavily, and his body began to shake. Then the cabin walls started to tremble.

Ori raised his voice, "That's enough! Stop or—"

"Or what?" Chivington asked. "There's nothing you can do, not in front of them."

"We've received special orders," Ori said. "Besides, they won't remember any of this. This will be spread across their psyches like a billion bits of fractured dreams. What they will remember is what we want them to remember."

Agent Chivington's mouth opened as if he was about to say something, but no words come out.

"It's time. Come willingly," Ori said as Vau, Tony, and Jordan surrounded Ego. "You know what will happen if you make me use force."

Slowly, the color drained from Chivington's face, and his shoulders slouched. "Why would you spend your energy on these creatures? You've witnessed the atrocities they've committed against their own brothers and sisters for rocks and paper."

"I still have faith that they can fulfill what they were created to do," Ori said.

With that, Tony, Vau, and Jordan escorted Agent Chivington out of the shack.

Jordan paused in front of Section Chief Appleton, staring into his eyes. "You'll see your fate soon enough."

Chapter 52

Section Chief Appleton slowly tested the back-door handle of Nicolas's house, expecting it to be locked. To his surprise, the knob turned easily, and he walked right in.

He was certain it was Nicolas who gave them up to Ori. Fortunately, he was still able to get out unscathed, but Nicolas would pay.

Although the house was dark, he could still see the piles of trash in Nicolas's place. It looked like a squatter had settled in. He heard the TV and slowly started walking down the hall, carefully pulling his Glock .45 ACP from the holster.

He approached the living room, allowing the blue light from the TV to illuminate his path. He raised his pistol slightly, preparing to point directly at the couch where he expected to find Nicolas. However, he found the couch vacant.

He grabbed the remote control and silenced the TV. He froze to listen intently, thinking that he heard a sound. He slowly turned his head to look behind him and saw a dark figure. Before he had time to react, he felt a hard hit to his head, and everything went black.

Feeling groggy, Jeremy started to open his eyes. The room was dim, lit only by a pale orange glow coming from a distant light. He was alone in this unfamiliar cell of a room. His stomach growled, and he wondered how much time had passed. He tried to move his hands and found that his wrists and ankles were bound with shackles. Metal chains led from the shackles to a thick steel ring on the ground.

He shouted with as much bravado as he could muster, "Hey! Where am I? Do you know who you are messing with?" He paused, waiting for a response. He heard some noise in the distance. It sounded like someone was scrubbing the floors. He tried again, "Hey, I know you hear me! Where am I? You better let me go, or you will be sorry!"

The scrubbing stopped, and he heard footsteps walking his way.

"Hello, Jeremy," a man with a light Latino accent said. His voice was steady and almost soothing. "Is everything okay?"

The man's voice had a gentle and friendly tone, which was surprising.

Confused and mad, Jeremy responded, "Does it look like everything's okay? You don't know who you are screwing with. I recommend that you get me out of here as soon as possible, or else it'll be your ass."

"Oh, don't worry, friend; we know exactly who you are. And what you've done." The man stepped closer, right in the light, as if he was allowing the section chief to recognize his face. He was a clean-shaven, well-groomed man. He was wearing a long, plastic apron that reached from his chest to his shoes. In his right hand, he held a white scrub brush with bristles the color of rust. "Our mutual friend, Nicolas, paid us a little visit here not too long ago. He had some amazing stories to tell."

Appleton thought to himself, *No, can't be.*

The aproned man tilted his head down. "My boss does not enjoy being used. To make matters worse, you forced his daughter into this ugly business of ours. Then you tried to have her killed?" The man paused and shook his head from side to side. "Shame, shame, shame, Jeremy."

"Nicolas is a snake. You can't believe a word he says," Jeremy pleaded.

The doctor looked at him evenly. "Ah, well, you will be two snakes in the grass, but with all venom removed. Let's begin, shall we?"

The Recruiter

Alexander Mukte

Acknowledgements

Thank you to my family and friends who have shown me nothing but support throughout this journey. I'd like to give a special thank you to the following people:

My courageous mom, Reachel. Thank you for helping to keep me motivated, especially near the end of this process.

My amazing editors and in-laws, Dr. Penny Ferguson and Awesome Sam. Your enthusiasm, support, and expertise were invaluable.

My loving wife and life partner, Julie, for always being wise, thoughtful, and supportive. Your patience and open-mindedness were critical in helping me turn this story in my head into a story that can be read by others. Without you, none of this would have been possible.

Alexander Mukte

About the Author

Alexander had an active imagination his whole life, but it wasn't until the birth of his son that he began putting the stories in his mind on paper. He wanted to be an example for his son of someone pursuing his passion, dreaming big, and taking chances.

Alexander loves people, their stories, and their backgrounds as well as what shapes them, how they think, and what they dream about. He has a passion for learning and is known by most as an intensely curious person who eagerly soaks up anything and everything he can. He dreamt of a career that allowed him to learn new things and meet new people every day. In writing, he has found a life that allows him to do just that.

The Recruiter is Alexander's first novel. We hope you enjoy it as much as we have.

Alexander Mukte

The Recruiter
Alexander Mukte

This readers group guide for The Recruiter includes an introduction, discussion questions, and ideas for enhancing your book club. The questions are intended to help your reading group find new and interesting angles and topics for discussion. We hope that these ideas will enrich your conversation and increase your enjoyment of the book.

Introduction

Leslie may be an idealist, but she's no fool. She trusts her boss, Ori, implicitly. When a bomb is detonated at work, she finds herself caught up in a whirlwind of events. Is Ori who she thinks he is? Why would anyone want to hurt him? And how do they get out of this mess? Leslie doesn't have it all figured out, but what becomes clear is that there's a lot the world doesn't know about Ori Clayborn.

1. After the FBI casts suspicion on Ori, did you doubt him, or did you doubt the FBI? Why?

2. If you were Leslie, would you have trusted Ori and have escaped with him? Or would you have stayed behind with authorities?

3. At what point did you realize Ori was African American? Did that adjust how you thought about him?

4. Mikiko & Evelyn are two strong women colleagues who help each other and trust each other. Is this normal? Do you experience or see this often at your work?

5. There are some highly capable, powerful women in this book. Do you think women carry their power differently than men? Do you think powerful men and women are perceived and judged differently?

6. Have you heard of imposter syndrome? Have you ever experienced it? Why might Leslie have been surprised that Ori saw so much strength and potential in her?

7. At Professor Raziel's house, did you see any themes in the books and artwork there? Why do you think the author chose what he did?

8. Do you think media today contains enough truth? Or is it biased? How has this changed how you consume news?

9. Do you believe Silas is good despite what he's done? Do you always follow orders from authority? When do you question?

10. What do you make of Senator Whitman? Did you understand his motives? Do you think things shifted for him at some point along the way?

Alexander Mukte